S0-BLG-739

He couldn't resist...

Nicky was trembling against him. Flint wrapped his arms around her. His heart pounded—partly from anxiety for her safety, but mostly from the attraction he'd somehow managed to deny for too long. When she raised her frightened face to his, a single tear visible, he did the only thing possible.

He kissed her.

Not a peck on the forehead or a brush across her lips, but a real, man-to-woman connection. Her mouth was soft...sweet...salty.... He could no longer tell where he ended and Nicky began. She stole his breath away, put wings to his soul.

He loosened his grip and took a step back, clenching his jaw. "Sorry," he muttered. "I guess I got carried away."

Nicky nodded, averting her gaze as if she couldn't bear to look directly at him. "Carried away by the... unusual circumstances."

So they were agreed. Why did that make him feel so lousy?

Dear Reader,

A hero or heroine without any faults would make pretty dull reading since the most gripping conflicts come, not from outside forces, but from within.

The Seven Deadly Sins—Pride, Sloth, Lust, Greed, Anger, Envy and Gluttony—exemplify the most hurtful behavior, human failings that can keep us locked in self-absorption and self-doubt. They can keep us from finding real happiness within ourselves...or with that one special person whom we all deserve...

As a writer, I love nothing more than throwing my heroes and heroines to the precipice of danger, to make ordinary people fight the worst villains and win. For me, it's a celebration of the human spirit, the discovery of untapped strengths that I am certain we all possess if only we can find the courage to reach deep inside ourselves.

For SEVEN SINS, I've chosen to raise the stakes, to push my heroes and heroines to the emotional edge at the same time they are fighting for their very existence. In the midst of mortal danger, they must wrestle with equally destructive inner demons and take back their lives...and in doing so, be rewarded with a love for all time.

Let me know how you enjoy their stories at P.O. Box 578279, Chicago, IL 60657-8297.

Patricia Rosemoor

After the Dark
Patricia Rosemoor

Harlequin Books

TORONTO • NEW YORK • LONDON
AMSTERDAM • PARIS • SYDNEY • HAMBURG
STOCKHOLM • ATHENS • TOKYO • MILAN
MADRID • WARSAW • BUDAPEST • AUCKLAND

If you purchased this book without a cover you should be aware
that this book is stolen property. It was reported as "unsold and
destroyed" to the publisher, and neither the author nor the
publisher has received any payment for this "stripped book."

Thanks to Dr. Rosalind Cartwright,
Director of Sleep Disorder Center,
Rush-Presbyterian-St. Luke's Medical Center
in Chicago, for the valuable information she shared
with me on sleep disorders.
Any inaccuracies—intended or otherwise—in the
depiction of Flint's disorder are mine.

ISBN 0-373-22451-6

AFTER THE DARK

Copyright © 1998 by Patricia Pinianski

All rights reserved. Except for use in any review, the reproduction or
utilization of this work in whole or in part in any form by any electronic,
mechanical or other means, now known or hereafter invented, including
xerography, photocopying and recording, or in any information storage
or retrieval system, is forbidden without the written permission of the
publisher, Harlequin Enterprises Limited, 225 Duncan Mill Road,
Don Mills, Ontario, Canada M3B 3K9.

All characters in this book have no existence outside the imagination of
the author and have no relation whatsoever to anyone bearing the same
name or names. They are not even distantly inspired by any individual
known or unknown to the author, and all incidents are pure invention.

This edition published by arrangement with Harlequin Books S.A.

® and TM are trademarks of the publisher. Trademarks indicated with
® are registered in the United States Patent and Trademark Office, the
Canadian Trade Marks Office and in other countries.

Printed in U.S.A.

PRIDE

AVARICE

WRATH

LUST

SEVEN DEADLY SINS

ENVY

GLUTTONY

SLOTH

SLOTH is a state of dejection
that leads to despair and faintheartedness.
A dispiriting sorrow so weighs upon
a person's mind that s/he sees no reason to act.
S/he denies that we are our brother's keeper.
S/he is empty of spirit.

CAST OF CHARACTERS

Flint Armstrong—He assumed he must be guilty...though he didn't remember a thing.

Nicky Keating—Believing in his innocence, Flint's sister-in-law was determined to prove it.

Beverly Jensen—Flint found the assistant state attorney dead in his bed.

Eric Jensen—The abusive ex-husband ignored the restraining order that was supposed to keep him away from Beverly.

Hector Villada—The violent criminal who held a grudge against the assistant state attorney was paroled the week before she died.

Sid Shelton—The unsavory businessman held a costly grudge against Flint.

Cecilia Keating—Nicky's mother held Flint responsible for the death of her older daughter and grandchild.

Oren Maticek—Cecilia's new beau seemed willing to do anything for her.

Prologue

A hot and humid summer evening meant the streets of Washington's Adams-Morgan neighborhood were ripe with aromas of exotic foods and noisy with the cacophony of foreign tongues. Mouth dry, Zoe Declue shouldered her way through the crowd, past Ethiopian and Salvadoran sidewalk cafés, rummage stores and funky galleries, Andean pipers and a bucket-drum combo.

Though the research psychologist in her was fascinated by the colorful if edgy area, dressed as she was in a tailored cream linen suit and matching pumps, Zoe feared she stuck out like a sore thumb. Not that clothes were the defining medium...she imagined Alex Gotham fit right in no matter what he wore.

Turning a corner onto a side street, she smoothed out the scrap of paper that she'd clutched into a ball and checked his address. His apartment had to be on the next block.

Since beginning their collaboration on *Seven Deadly Sins*—a humanistic look at Pride, Envy, Wrath, Sloth, Avarice, Gluttony and Lust—they'd been meeting at her DuPont Circle offices. But that afternoon, Alex had failed to show. When she'd called him, he'd claimed he was under the weather. Zoe had been tempted to accept the explanation, but some instinct had made her push until he'd agreed to meet after hours at his place.

His redbrick apartment house was stately and well groomed. The doorway windows sparkled and wood paneling in the vestibule smelled of lemon polish. Chest tight, she buzzed Alex. Something was wrong and she wanted to know what. This book was the most important thing in her life.

A few moments later, she came face-to-face with the sometime reporter who held her life in his hands. As usual, he was dressed in dark trousers and matching collarless shirt. But his clothes were wrinkled and his thick black hair tousled around his face. Not a good sign. Not good at all. And though a smile creased his mouth, his deep brown eyes were shuttered as they studied her.

"Can I come in?"

He stood aside. Brushing past him, she took a careful look around. His living space was large, open and enviable, but signs of neglect were everywhere, from the frayed lampshades to the dust collecting on the bookshelves, from the piles of newspapers on the floor to the coffee table where a bottle of whiskey sat open next to an empty tumbler.

The liquor gave her a start. If he had a problem with alcohol, that could explain why he'd never written another book after *Lost Youth*, his highly touted nonfiction look into the world of teenage runaways.

"I did warn you," Alex said, moving closer. "You should have worn those hip boots."

Though he appeared hungover, he didn't smell of

alcohol, and the characteristic tongue-in-cheek comment was promising.

"Why don't we sit," she suggested, taking the chair nearest the window. "I read the chapter on pride last night."

After he'd faxed the pages to her without first calling to say he'd finished.

Pacing, he asked, "And?"

Was he worried about her reaction? "As wonderful as I imagined it would be."

"You're sure?"

"Positive."

Alex fell onto the couch and picked up the whiskey bottle. Rather than pouring himself a drink, however, he replaced the cap.

Tension lifting from her shoulders, she asked, "So...are you ready to go on?"

"Hit me."

Zoe pulled a folder of research materials from her leather briefcase. The purpose of her project was to show how the emotion-based sins kept a person isolated from society and therefore from loving freely. And through the cooperation of colleagues and their patients across the country, she was able to focus on personal narratives. One example of someone who'd found a second chance at life for each chapter.

"This story is about a man filled with such despair that he can't force himself to take interest in anything," she began, "...not even if it means saving his own life."

Zoe wondered at his sudden, odd expression. Reluctance? But he covered it quickly and took the article she'd pulled from its file.

Zoe handed Alex an article. The headline: Earthquake Survivor Charged with Prosecutor's Murder.

Chapter One

Rumbling that started deep in the bowels of the earth penetrated his subconscious.

Then screams...echoes of hysteria.

He tossed and turned, attempting to vanquish the troubling din. But the bed, shifting with a violent twist and tilt, propelled him against the headboard, effectively demolishing his cocoon of sleep.

Eyes flashed open to blackness broken by bursts of lightning outside the bedroom windows. No, not lightning, his confused brain reasoned...transformers popping with an eerie electrical blue glow.

"Alana?"

No response. Alone. Where was she? Sleeping on the couch again?

The room's continued shaking toppled objects from their perches and smashed them against the walls and floor. Somewhere nearby, panicked voices jumbled together over the crack and splinter of glass.

Earthquake...

"Alana! Megan!"

Heart racing in panic, he flew from the bed. His feet hit the floor, then continued right through it as the room began collapsing in on itself. A whomp on the side of the head stunned him. Slowed him. Not for long. He had to get to his daughter. And his wife. Maybe Alana was already with Megan.

Maybe her absence had nothing to do with their fight.

Blindly clawing and crawling his way through the shifting rubble, walls and ceiling folding like a house of cards around him, he forced his way from the room.

"Alana...Megan!"

But his desperate shout prompted no answer.

Tremors receding, the earth suddenly went still, the eerie silence accompanied by a blasting wave of heat. Unable to tell whether the surrounding air had changed or adrenaline scorched his insides, he fought a threatening nausea.

A horrible wail from somewhere beyond their apartment and a faint if persistent call for help from another direction made the skin along his spine crawl. He was disoriented. Directionless. He wouldn't admit to powerless.

Pushing himself upright, he somehow stumbled several yards until his foot hit something soft just outside what had been his daughter's room.

A body.

A shaft of moonlight slashing through a break in the roof revealed his wife, open eyes staring at him...pleading with him...something dark streaking her high forehead and the pale red-gold hair spread around her delicate face.

"Alana, honey, thank God I found you." Dropping to his knees, he touched her gently. "I'll get you out of here, I promise. You and Megan."

Refusing to consider what he might find on the other side of the door to his daughter's room, he tried to free Alana first, but she was trapped by debris. No budging her. Nor could he find any signs of life. Bile filled his throat. She had to be alive. She and Megan. The alternative was unthinkable.

"Wake up...say something...please..."

He shook her, gently at first, then harder, desperately, as if force could bring a response.

"Alana! No-o-o..."

"ALANA!"

Covered in sweat, heart palpitating, Flint Armstrong awoke, still shaking her. His knees dug into the mattress, the flesh beneath his hands cool and unresponsive.

His head began clearing.

Not Alana. Alana was dead. Had been for nearly a year now. Then who?

He snapped on the nightstand light and took a good look at the person in his bed. Beverly Jensen...the woman he'd been seeing for several weeks. Dark hair spread across the pillow, she appeared peaceful.

Sleeping.

Dreaming.

But even before searching for her pulse, he knew.

Her head lolled to the side, reminding him of a broken doll. Fighting a panic attack, unable to take a normal breath, heart threatening to burst through the wall of his chest, Flint scrambled off her body. He stood next to the bed, his gaze fixed on the dead woman.

Trying to remember something—anything—about what had happened.

An image haunted him. Alana. Forehead and hair darkened by blood. Dead.

But that was before. Nearly a year ago. Not that he

could remember anything but that single image; he must have had some bizarre nightmare. Night terrors stirred from a childhood graveyard by the unbearable guilt of a night he didn't want to remember. A night he had no hopes of ever forgetting.

At least he'd known how his wife and child had died.

Now Beverly was equally dead...

Oblivious as to how long he stood there, Flint slowly absorbed the truth of the matter.

After which he picked up the telephone and dialed 911.

Even so, the voice on the other end had to prompt him several times before he finally found the words.

Voice raspy with growing despair, he said, "I want to report an untimely death...."

NICKY KEATING FETCHED her morning newspaper from the vestibule and climbed back to her second-floor apartment where she finished preparing a breakfast fit for a football player under the watchful eye of her best buddy.

"You know the rules," she told him as she worked. "No getting underfoot."

In response, Scraps merely yawned, then went back on alert. Flipping the potatoes, Nicky grinned. No matter how much she fed the mutt, he somehow managed to maintain his "hungry" look when people food was around.

Her kitchen was too small for anything but cooking. So, loading up a large tray, she muscled it into the dining room, the dog on her heels. Plates of eggs, sausage, hash browns, thick Greek toast, melon and freshly squeezed orange juice in addition to a small pot of French Roast coffee quickly covered half the table. Brass candlesticks and the huge red poinsettia her students had given her complemented the red and green tablecloth embellished with gold threads.

"Pretty festive, huh?"

Scraps barked once in agreement. She ruffled the dog's short brown and white fur, then sat.

Christmas had always been her favorite holiday, as the elaborately decorated tree twinkling at her from the living room attested. Ignoring the lone unclaimed package sitting beneath the lower branches, she poured herself a mug of coffee and inhaled half of the strong brew before digging into the eggs and potatoes.

Normally, she only went all-out for Sunday breakfast, but school being recessed for the holidays, she'd decided to treat herself every morning. A warm dog nose pressed to her knee reminded her someone else expected a treat, as well.

"Don't you know begging isn't dignified?"

Scraps didn't seem to care. He whistled pitifully. Laughing, Nicky shared a sausage with him, then ladled samples of everything onto a smaller plate, which she set on the floor. His dish was licked clean before hers was half-empty...all but the melon, which he'd mouthed and spat out.

He was on the alert again.

"No more, Scraps," she said, giving him a couple of pats on the side and signaling him to lie down.

He followed orders without complaint. Amazing how much he'd learned in the few months she'd had him.

A few more bites and her hunger abated. She could finish at a more leisurely pace while reading the newspaper, which she'd left on a side table. About to pull

out the sports section—as a physical education
teacher, she kept abreast with team scores and name
players so her high school students didn't have one
over her—she hesitated when she glanced at the front-
page headline: Earthquake Survivor Charged with
Prosecutor's Murder.

Her pulse surged and instinct put a name to the
accused man, even before her gaze dropped to the photograph, taken at a political gathering, that accompanied the article. Dark hair a little too shaggy, pale eyes
haunted, Flint appeared to be forcing a smile at Beverly Jensen.

Heart in her throat, Nicky read the copy with growing disbelief, absorbed the bare facts with difficulty.

*Beverly dead on Christmas Eve...Flint alerting
the authorities...the arrest...his not remembering...
neither admitting nor denying responsibility...*

Police maintained there was no possibility of homicide by misadventure, no accidental death. Physical
evidence had proved that, following a struggle in the
dining room where she'd received the fatal injury that
had broken her neck, Beverly Jensen had been dragged
to Flint's bed.

Stunned, Nicky lowered the paper.

While Flint had refused to sign a confession, he'd
done nothing on his own behalf, either. The court had
appointed a public defender to see him through the
hearing. A high bond had been set, in accordance with
the first-degree-murder charge, though Flint hadn't
taken that option. Knowing his financial circumstances
weren't the best these days, Nicky figured he might
not be able to raise the money.

So why hadn't he called one of his old friends?
Or her?

Rather than asking for help, he chose confinement to a Cook County jail cell, chose to remain a pawn of the capricious justice system.

Because he was guilty?

She couldn't...wouldn't...*didn't* believe it.

A loud peal startled her. Scraps sat up and whined in response to the doorbell. A series of impatient blasts followed. Someone was in a big hurry. Dropping the newspaper, Nicky stumbled to her front door, the dog following closely.

Her numb fingers fumbled over the intercom button. "Who is it?"

"Who are you expecting at this time of the morning?" came the shrill reply.

"Mom."

Heart sinking, suspecting her mother already knew about Flint, she hit the buzzer. If only they could share some concern over him...but she knew better.

Fingercombing the spikes of her flame-red hair, Nicky wished she had time to change out of the oversize glittery sweatshirt and leggings she was wearing. Her mother had never been one to hide her opinions. Nicky opened the door just as the older woman rushed up the final few stairs. Scraps took one look at their visitor and retreated.

"Morning, Mom."

"Nicole."

Cecilia Keating turned her cheek to accept Nicky's kiss, then continued into the living room. She removed the fur that had seen better years and flung it over the back of the couch. As long as Nicky could remember, that coat had been a symbol of the lifestyle her mother believed she'd been meant to lead. The sleek designer dress in a clear green added to the illusion of substance. Occasional jobs as a party planner barely kept the wolf from her door.

Hoping this unexpected appearance was more innocent than she suspected, Nicky kept her tone light. "Out shopping for after-Christmas sales so early?"

She wished her mother would agree, would tell her she was looking for something dishy to wear for that new man she'd recently started dating. Nicky had found out there *was* a man, though she still didn't know his name or anything about him.

"Don't be sarcastic with me." Her mother gave her glitzy casual outfit a disapproving frown but kept from commenting. Then her gaze wandered to the dining room table where it fixed on the discarded *Chicago Tribune.* "I assume you've read the dreadful news."

"It is horrible—"

"I only hope our names aren't brought up in connection with that man's. How humiliating that would be."

Nicky crossed her arms over her chest. "*That man* is your son-in-law."

"Not anymore." Her mother turned to her, eyes shining with unshed tears. "Bless your sister's soul. This only goes to prove what I've been saying all along."

Nicky swallowed hard. "Flint was not responsible for Alana and Megan's deaths, Mom—"

"He's the one who insisted they move to Los Angeles!"

"—and he didn't murder Beverly Jensen."

"You don't know that."

"I know *him.*"

Her mother threw up her hand, waving away Nicky's statement as inconsequential. "When he forced his way into Alana's life, you were too young to properly evaluate his character. He infatuated you almost as much as he did your sister. In your eyes, he never did any wrong.''

An old argument, one that increasingly got on Nicky's nerves. She couldn't stop herself. ''What wrong did Flint do...other than marry your favored daughter and loosen your grasp on her a little?''

Cecilia caught her breath and stepped back. ''Nicole, if you cannot speak to me with civility, do not speak to me at all.'' She actually looked hurt.

And Nicky acknowledged the stirrings of guilt. Would she never learn to think before she opened her mouth?

''I don't want to argue, Mom. Especially not during the holidays.''

Especially not after the wonderful Christmas they'd just shared. She'd felt they'd gotten truly close for the first time in her twenty-six years—the best gift anyone could have given her. She didn't want to spoil the magic.

''You're right. We must stick together. We only have each other now.''

Her mother wrapped her arms around Nicky, who could hardly swallow past the lump in her throat. She returned the embrace with an extra-hard squeeze, then stepped back before she started sniffling like a kid.

''Hey, want some breakfast?'' she asked, indicating what was left of the spread on the dining room table. ''This stuff is cold, but I have more of everything. It'll only take a few minutes.''

''No, dear, but thank you. I've been eating too much because of the holidays as it is.''

Not that anyone would know it. At fifty, Cecilia

Keating had the figure of a woman twenty years her junior...as Alana had been. Not for the first time, Nicky mused that her sister had been her mother's younger reflection, both being moderately tall and naturally willowy, with delicate features, green eyes and red-gold hair...though her mother's was now lightened becomingly by an increasing number of silver threads.

While Nicky had her golf-pro father's love of anything sports related, she sometimes wished she could skip some of the daily aerobic activity necessary to keep her more plush shape from spreading out of control. But then, unlike her sister, she'd always had to put forth extra effort, whether it was to look good or to get something she wanted. Nothing came easily to her. As often as not, she didn't even get close.

The mental comparison generated a discomfiting sense of disloyalty to her late sister. Nicky started stacking dishes on the tray.

"So, Mom, what are you up to today?"

"The question is...what are *you?*"

Figuring Flint was *the* reason for her mother's visit, she kept her focus on clearing the table. "You have something in mind?"

"I want to know what you intend to do about that man."

Nicky sighed. She hadn't had enough time to think things through, but she couldn't sit around and twiddle her thumbs. Not that her mother would want to hear that.

"Maybe we shouldn't talk about Flint."

"I knew it. You're going to see him, aren't you? You're going to involve yourself in this scandal."

Reputation over everything. Nicky wasn't surprised. "You can't expect me to abandon him. He's family."

"He's no such thing!"

"Fine." Stopping the busywork, she faced her indignant mother. "So you disown him. I don't. I can't sit around pretending nothing is wrong when my sister's husband is in trouble." She softened her tone. "You of all people should understand...Alana would want us to stick by Flint."

Cecilia shook her head and closed her eyes. When she opened them again, the anger was gone, replaced by something not as readily identifiable.

"Stay away from him, Nicole, please. *For me.*"

All her life, she'd tried to please her mother. Not that it had seemed to matter when her sister was around. *Alana, the perfect daughter...* Unexpectedly finding herself an only child meant Nicky had had another chance at bonding with her emotionally distant parent. But no matter how much that meant to her, she couldn't go against her own principles.

"I'm sorry, I can't make any such promise."

"You would twist a knife in my heart?"

The tension making her more uncomfortable by the moment, Nicky said, "Try to understand this isn't about you. Now please drop it."

Her mother's expression closed. "Fine. Then I'll leave you to your plans."

"Mom—"

Spinning on her high heels, Cecilia rushed back into the living room and swept up her fur, then headed straight for the door.

"Mom, you don't have to go."

But she watched her mother exit as if she hadn't heard, without so much as a goodbye.

Nicky's eyes stung as she grabbed the newspaper and marched into the living room. There she threw herself into a big tattered upholstered chair that was her favorite, maybe because it was all she had of her father. Scraps magically reappeared to keep her company as she reread the nightmare of a story. By the time she finished, her own feelings were under tight control, and she was ready to do whatever was necessary to get Flint out of this mess.

First on the agenda…she had to find out how to go about arranging his release.

THE SUN WAS SETTING by the time Nicky pulled her Escort through the gates of the Cook County mega-facility at Twenty-Sixth and California. It had taken most of the day and all her resources—including calling in a few favors—to raise the required ten percent of Flint's bond.

She'd even drained a savings account that her parents had opened for her when she was a child, one that had been left jointly in her and her mother's name after her father had walked out on them. The account had actually been meant as a college fund. Independent as always, Nicky had worked her way through school, leaving the account untouched in case of an emergency.

This was an emergency.

Having drained the healthy balance, she only hoped she'd have the wherewithal to replace the money before her mother found out she'd used it for Flint—surely she'd have a stroke.

Not that Nicky was worried about losing the money. Flint wouldn't skip out of town to avoid going to trial when he hadn't even fought for his own release.

Though Flint Armstrong was alive, he hadn't really survived the earthquake. His spirit had been buried in the rubble that had taken his family. He'd come back to Chicago a shattered man. Nicky sometimes thought returning to the house where he'd made a life with Alana and Megan had been a big mistake. He wasn't recovering from his grief.

And she didn't know what to think about his affair with Beverly...

Gray sky added to piles of dirty snow in the parking lot made the stark buildings of the county facility appear even more grim. Razor wire threaded through and topped the twelve-foot chain link fencing, and sniper towers located at regular intervals as far as she could see turned dark eyes on those who challenged the justice system's gates.

The place simply gave Nicky the creeps.

Before she could lose her nerve, she headed for the doors. Inside, she passed through the security station, glad for the metal detector that stopped other callers from bringing in weapons. Many of the visitors hanging around the lobby could very well be miscreants, the only difference between them and the inmates being that these hadn't been caught....

She couldn't imagine a man like Flint incarcerated in a horrible place that housed thousands of real criminals. She was doubly glad she hadn't caved in to her mother's demands.

She only hoped she wouldn't have cause to regret her decision.

FLINT LAY on his narrow cot, the din of other inmates socializing in the common area adjoining the double tiers of cells barely penetrating his consciousness. He was concentrating, trying to force memories where there were none.

He'd gone over that last evening with Beverly again and again. They'd been at a Christmas Eve party but had come home early. He hadn't gotten drunk on two beers, but he might as well have been. For, no matter how hard he tried, he couldn't make a connection with the time between falling into bed and waking with Beverly's lifeless body in his grasp. They hadn't argued. He had no earthly reason to want to hurt her.

But obviously he had.

Being charged with her murder had seemed like a perversion of the justice that he'd escaped for nearly a year. It had been almost a relief to give in to his fate.

And yet...

He hadn't been able to bring himself to sign a confession to something he didn't remember doing...when the only image that stuck in his mind was that of his late wife.

He'd experienced several similar incidents in the past few months, waking in a state of panic, a lifeless Alana clear in his mind. His wife...but not his daughter, thank God. He couldn't even think about Megan without his heart breaking all over again. The mischievous four year-old had been the center of his universe. But he couldn't tolerate thinking about her. Even now, he forced away the image of her impish face topped by a riot of red-gold curls. He'd done inexplicable things in his sleep. Throwing a chair across the room one time. Breaking a lamp another. Frightening the stray dog he'd given a home into hiding under an end table from him.

This was the first time he'd awakened in bed rather

than in some other part of the house. Thankfully, it was also the first body.

So, had he had some violent nightmare he couldn't remember but had acted out, accidentally killing Beverly?

Shouting from the tier startled him out of his deliberation. A couple of inmates having a disagreement. Which was quickly broken up by a guard. Nothing unusual. The past few days had been a waking nightmare.

Not that being arrested had come as a surprise. And he'd been prepared for what would follow...or so he'd thought.

Originally jailed at the station house, he'd been numb waiting for the print to clear while the State's Attorney's Office had been running a felony review on him. Then he'd been brought to Cook County for a bond hearing where formal charges had been brought against him. Considering Beverly had been an assistant state's attorney, the judge's setting bond at all had surprised him. While his readily available funds weren't exactly healthy, he had quite a bit of equity in his home, and he probably could have gotten a quick loan.

He hadn't been able to bring himself to do anything about that, either.

Being incarcerated was undoubtedly what he deserved, but each day brought new reason for further retreat. If this was the real world, he'd be better off leaving it....

"Armstrong," called a guard from the tier. "This is your lucky day."

"How so?"

The uniformed man stepped into the doorway of his

cell, which remained open most of the day. "You've been sprung."

"Cleared?"

Had some new information come to light?

"Hell, no. Someone's bailed you out."

Flint started. "Who?"

"Ain't none of my never mind." More shouts from the tier caught the guard's attention. Glancing behind him, he said, "Get your butt in gear and find out for yourself," before going to investigate.

Numbly, Flint rose from the bunk, trying to figure out who would go to such trouble for him. Such expense. And him with no family nearby. He was an only child and his mother was dead. Although his father was alive, a decade ago he'd retired to Arizona after remarrying. Lewis Armstrong was approaching eighty and not in the best of health. Flint had been hoping that the news wouldn't get to his dad, and the likelihood that it had was slim.

Who, then, was his champion?

One of his old business partners?

Flint couldn't feature it. He hadn't been in contact with either Terrence Clarke or Linda Torres since first returning from L.A., when they'd made overtures that he'd ignored.

Only one other name sprang to mind.

Nicky Keating had the crazy notion that supporting him was necessary because of her loyalty to Alana and Megan. In truth, he'd always thought of her as the sister he'd never had. Because he was fond of Nicky, he hadn't wanted his misery after the earthquake to bring her down.

A good kid who took her obligations too seriously, she'd inserted herself into his life without permission anyway. She kept track of him. Made sure he ate. Seemed to have a sixth sense about his moods. When he'd realized Scraps would be better off at an animal shelter than with him, she'd even insisted on giving the poor mutt a home. Only lately had she backed off.

By the time he changed into his street clothes, took possession of his effects and signed some forms, Flint figured at least an hour had slipped by. He'd been finding it more and more difficult to keep track. To stay focused.

When the last locked door was opened to him, he immediately looked for Nicky on the other side.

She was waiting for him.

Because she didn't spot him immediately, for a moment he watched her in silence. Sometimes he wondered at her being the sister of the sleek and complicated woman who had been his wife.

Short and cute, Nicky resembled a Christmas elf in her sparkly sweatshirt, leggings and ankle boots. She was pacing, fingering the red spikes of her hair with short nails painted the same deep violet that tinted her eyelids and lips. And if he weren't mistaken, those lips were doing a bit of mumbling.

Giving herself a pep talk so she could bring herself to deal with him?

Flint might have smiled...but wasted lives left him nothing to smile about.

As if sensing his silent approach, Nicky turned. He noted the strain of uncertainty making her baby face appear more mature. Her blue eyes were wide with apprehension. She was waiting for his reaction.

His approval.

Flint couldn't bring himself to give her what she wanted.

Instead, he asked, "When are you going to learn to use the good sense you were born with?" more harshly than he'd meant to. She got enough criticism from her witch of a mother.

And Nicky's expression, going straight from disappointment to disgust, gave him another shot of guilt to tie up his gut.

Chapter Two

She should have known better than to think she'd get a lick of gratitude from Flint, Nicky groused to herself as he stared at her out of spooky gray eyes. She forced a smile to cover her discomfort. And worry. He wasn't looking too good. A few days in a jail cell and the cotton pullover and trousers seemed to bag on his lanky frame, as if he'd lost more weight. Equally scary, his skin already held a prison pallor that accentuated the ragged scar slashing through one thick eyebrow, a souvenir of the earthquake.

Or maybe she was imagining the differences. She couldn't actually remember the last time he'd looked like himself.

Hating the silence between them, Nicky said, "Nice to see you, too."

Flint drew closer, his greater height obliging her to tilt her head to keep eye contact.

"I don't understand," he finally said. "You couldn't possibly afford tens of thousands to cover my bond. Where did you get the money?"

"I robbed a bank." The fake smile went sour. "And you're welcome."

Irritated, she grabbed her stadium jacket from the

back of a chair and started to leave. No sooner did she tell herself she didn't care if he followed than she sensed him directly behind her. His silence shouted volumes. No doubt she was nuts for bailing Flint's sorry butt out of jail.

"You didn't have to do this, Nicky."

"I know."

Poking her arms into the jacket, she pushed through the door and braved the cold before zipping up. The sun was down, the temperature dropping. He was right beside her, his stride easily matching hers.

"I didn't ask for your help."

"You never ask for anyone's help," she snapped, shoving her hands into leather gloves.

"You didn't go to a loan shark, did you?"

The ridiculous assumption added speed to her gait. "Maybe I won the lottery."

His hooking her upper arm brought her to a sudden stop on an icy patch that almost put her off her feet. Flint steadied her with both hands as he made her face him.

"I don't know why or how…but thank you…not that you should have."

Nicky sighed and caved. How could she stay angry with a man who was so down he thought he deserved to rot in prison rather than have someone lend him a hand?

"Let's get you out of here, huh?"

"To where?"

"Not to your place, that's for sure. The police secured it as a crime scene."

"A cheap motel—"

"Is not what I had in mind." She figured she'd

better inch him into the situation. "Besides, first things first."

"I suppose that means food."

"You know me too well."

"I've had years of practice."

An entire decade's worth, Nicky realized, leading the way to her car. Sometimes she felt as if Flint had been part of her life forever. Other times, she thought she didn't know *this* Flint at all.

"I managed to miss lunch. You don't mind an early dinner?"

"Whatever."

Ignoring his lack of enthusiasm, Nicky thought back to the holidays exactly ten years before, to the first time Alana had brought Flint home to meet her family.

He'd been different then. Oh, so different. And not merely in looks, which had been great enough to weaken any girl's knees. He'd had a crazy sense of humor. A warmth that had drawn in everyone he met. Everyone but her mother, she amended. But most attractive of all, he'd had an incredible zest for life— for celebrating every moment to its fullest—that she'd been unable to resist.

That was the biggest, most disheartening change in him.

Since losing his family, Flint didn't seem to care what fate had in store for him. But *she* cared, Nicky thought. She always had, practically from the moment he'd set foot in their house. Ten years ago, she'd been different, too. Young. Naive. Too openhearted.

And she'd fallen madly in love with her sister's new boyfriend.

His suddenly asking, "Did you forget what your car looks like?" startled her.

"What?"

"You passed it up back there." He thumbed her in the correct direction.

Flushing, Nicky did a quick turnabout and swept by him, not stopping until she reached the Escort. She unlocked both doors and climbed behind the wheel, immediately starting the engine and turning on the heat.

"It should be warm in a few minutes."

If Flint heard, he didn't comment. He was staring out the side window at the closest sniper tower. Nicky chose to let him be. For the moment. She wanted to get him away from the depressing place as fast as possible.

Once out of the lot, her mind wandered back to the past.

Thankfully, teenage crushes didn't last, and she'd gotten over her romantic delusions when Alana had become engaged to Flint. She'd continued to care about him, of course, but in a more proper way. As she'd told her mother earlier, he was family. Almost like a brother to her. It was only natural that she'd worry about Flint and go to bat for him when he was in trouble.

Not that he seemed to appreciate her efforts.

Over the past months, his resisting her at every turn had kept her from pushing too hard. She'd picked her battles, had backed off when retreat had seemed the wisest course. She'd figured that, more than anything, he needed time to heal. But that didn't seem to be happening, and time wouldn't do a thing for his current situation.

Nicky knew that, if she weren't willing to go the

distance—no matter how much fight Flint put up—she might as well quit before she got started.

HIS HOUSE WAS a dark spot capping a row of elaborately lit holiday displays. Flint barely caught a glimpse of the place as they drove over the bridge that crossed the narrow North Branch of the Chicago River.

House...not home.

The brown brick bungalow had hardly been a real home anymore when they'd left for California. Now the walls supplied him with nothing but shelter. A place to lay down his head at night. He really ought to get rid of it. Anything available in Ravenswood Manor was snapped up quickly, and he would be able to get a decent selling price, especially since his property was directly on the river itself.

At least he could give Nicky her money back, Flint thought, worrying about her source of cash. *If* he were allowed to sell, considering the circumstances.

"We're here," she announced.

They pulled in front of the apartment house that sat little more than two blocks from his place. She'd found her apartment right after landing her teaching position. He'd been glad to see her get away from Cecilia. Not that *Nicky* had ever been under her mother's thumb.

He followed her inside and up the stairs to her door decorated with a simple wreath of twigs, pinecones and a single sparkly ribbon. He couldn't miss the excited whine coming from inside. When Nicky opened the door, the warmth and scents of the holiday escaped into the hallway, along with the dog, who danced around her feet.

"Good boy, Scraps." Nicky ruffled the dog's ears and kissed him on the nose. "I bet you've got to go *outside*."

Her emphasis on the last whipped the mutt around to a basket that held his leash. The next thing Flint knew, Scraps fetched and dragged the leather lead toward them, the metal clasp clanking along the wooden floor.

Attaching one end of the leash to the dog's collar, Nicky held out the other. "You take him while I raid the fridge."

Flint hesitated until Scraps nudged his leg and made a silly familiar sound deep in his throat. Melting brown eyes were fixed on his face, and a wide yawn escaped the pointed nose—his way of telling Flint he really had to go *now*. It seemed the mutt didn't hold grudges.

"All right." He took the leash. "Come on, boy. Let's go for a walk."

With a short bark of excitement, Scraps led the way. Flint caught a glimpse of Nicky's grin before he was dragged down the stairs.

Nicky was good for him. He knew that. She lit a candle in his dark soul. So why couldn't he more readily take the hand of friendship that she offered him?

Once outside, he inhaled deeply, not minding the cold. The air was fresh, untainted by the stale odor of imprisonment. Even the alley they strolled seemed welcoming in comparison to his jail cell.

How had he gotten so low?

For more months than he cared to count, he'd done little more than go through the motions. Getting up in the mornings...going to some meaningless job in collections when he managed to find temporary skip-tracing work…eating alone…existing on memories and guilt.

His finding a scruffy, hungry, homeless mutt down by the river had given him purpose. He'd taken better care of Scraps than he had of himself. In return, he'd received unconditional love and much-needed companionship for several weeks. And then had come the incident that triggered Flint into giving up the dog for his own good.

Afterward, he'd been lonelier than before…the main reason he'd hooked up with Beverly, he guessed. A bad basis on which to start a relationship. Selfish on his part. Potentially hurtful to her.

Realizing that, he'd determined to end it.

But more than a week had gone by without his finding the energy to broach the subject. If he had…

Beverly was now out of his life, all right. Permanently. His fault.

And Nicky was still insisting on being there for him, no matter that she'd gotten little gratitude. If he let her stick around long enough, she, too, could get hurt. Something Flint knew his conscience couldn't handle.

But without her to light the way once in a while, he might as well be in the dark forever.

NICKY HAD BEEN RIGHT about the walk with Scraps relaxing Flint. He seemed more at ease as they polished off her leftover turkey and trimmings. Hopefully, he'd be more open to the assistance she was determined to force on him if necessary. She'd already taken the first step by making an important telephone call while he'd been out.

Because she chose to avoid discussing his legal fix for the moment, she shared some amusing stories about her students instead. Afterward, they cleaned up together. Then Nicky shooed Flint into the living room.

Following a few minutes later with homemade cookies and mugs of freshly brewed coffee, she was brought up short by the sight of him with that morning's *Tribune*. His grim visage sent unease crawling through her stomach.

"Catching up on your reading?" she asked, purposely keeping her tone light.

Flint immediately folded the newspaper, which he threw onto the couch cushion next to him. "Enlightening to see how reporters connect the dots."

Nicky set the plate on the coffee table and handed him a mug before curling up in her chair. She sipped at her coffee, waiting for him to enlighten her. When talking about the article didn't seem to be on his agenda, she indicated the lone present under the Christmas tree.

"That's yours, you know. I was hoping to give it to you on Christmas Eve."

Though she'd invited him to come by, he hadn't actually agreed. And in the end, he'd chosen to spend the night with Beverly Jensen.

His mistake.

"I got otherwise involved," he muttered, staring at the present. "And I didn't do any shopping this year."

"I wasn't expecting anything in return. Feel free to find out what's inside."

"Maybe later." When he turned his gaze on her, his eyes were devoid of expression. "Right now we need to get a few things straight about my situation."

Relieved that she hadn't had to introduce the topic

herself, Nicky took a long swallow of coffee before launching into what she expected would be a debate.

"Fine. First of all, you're going to stay here until we can get the police to release your house."

"No."

"What? The single bed in my office doesn't appeal to you?"

"I won't involve you in—"

"I'm involving myself," Nicky interrupted.

"Stop being so hardheaded."

"Maybe I will...when you stop being a martyr."

She caught her breath as color darkened his features and his jaw clenched. Finally. A reaction. How promising.

"I won't put you in danger!" he snapped.

"What kind of danger?"

"What if I don't stay in my own bed?"

Nicky's pulse picked up a beat, even though he didn't mean anything personal by that.

She knew all about his bizarre sleepwalking episodes. About his breaking things and not remembering. After he'd decided to give up Scraps, she'd forced the details out of him. And though they hadn't yet discussed it, she figured something similarly weird had gone down the night Beverly died.

Still, she said, "It's not likely, is it? Not when weeks go by between episodes."

"But it's nothing I can predict—"

"Then I'll take Scraps into the bedroom with me and I'll lock my door. Trust me. If you try knocking it down, I'll wake up fast."

"And then what? Chances are you couldn't wake *me.* Alana always said I could sleep through an earthquake."

His gaze locked with hers and Nicky sensed his surge of ire, not that it was directed at her. For a moment, she was able to cut through the gray shadows, to discern the force of personality she remembered as belonging to the real Flint. That this inimitable strength was merely buried rather than destroyed convinced her that he wasn't beyond hope.

Then he blinked and shut her out again.

Taking advantage of his mental retreat, she said, "Your staying here will be fine," with more confidence than she was feeling. "And it'll only be for a couple of days."

"Don't count on that. The authorities can secure a crime scene for as long as they want."

"Unless you get a good lawyer."

"I have a lawyer."

"What you have is an overworked, underpaid public defender," she countered, bolstering her courage with the argument. "And, from what I can tell, she's green behind the ears. Handling a first-degree-murder case calls for a legal eagle with clout."

"Don't make this your problem."

"Your life may be on the line here."

"Some would say it's my karma."

Nicky didn't believe karma included punishing a man for a tragedy not of his own making. But Flint obviously did. Guilt was doing his thinking for him. His not dealing with his grief was dragging him down a dangerous road.

A fact that ticked her off good.

"You're not thinking straight, Flint. If you really had a death wish, you would have signed that confession!" she practically shouted, hoping to reengage his anger. Maybe that would get him off his mental butt.

"But you didn't. You couldn't even take responsibility for that."

"I couldn't confess to something I didn't remember doing," he calmly returned.

"So why didn't you contact a lawyer who would get to the truth of the matter?"

"If *I* can't get to the truth—"

"Why didn't you call *me?*"

Appalled, Nicky shut her big mouth. She hadn't meant to expose her hurt.

Flint sighed. "We're talking about murder here. You can't fix this, Nicky. No one can."

"You're not a murderer."

"Even though I pleaded *not guilty,* I did kill Beverly." He sounded grim. "I just don't happen to remember doing it."

"Then maybe you didn't."

"There's no other explanation."

Because it seemed likely, she didn't argue the point. "Even assuming you had something to do with Beverly's death, it had to be some kind of crazy accident...like what happened the night you scared Scraps into hiding from you."

"He got away. Beverly didn't. Murder is murder."

"Not necessarily."

"The justice system will decide."

That he was being so complacent about his fate galled her, even though she understood his reason—guilt, plain and simple. Mother Nature had claimed his wife and child but had spared him. He'd committed the grievous sin of survival and hadn't been able to forgive himself. Maybe he never would, at least not without professional trauma and grief counseling, which he had so far refused.

"Flint, you have to make an effort to get over what happened to Alana and Megan—"

"You want me to forget them?"

"Of course not! I know you'll always honor their memories. But their deaths were not your fault. You have to stop punishing yourself over something you couldn't control."

"I don't need this psychobabble."

"Yes, you do, but I'm not really qualified to give it to you. You need a professional. Excuse me...at the moment you need *two* professionals...." She seized the perfect opening to tell him what she had done. "That includes a top lawyer to handle your preliminary hearing tomorrow." She took a big breath and braced herself. "That's why I called Phelps Rendell on your behalf."

"You what? When?"

"Earlier this afternoon and then again while you were out walking Scraps to confirm. Mr. Rendell respects you, Flint, and he wants to help you if he can. He'll be here—" she checked her watch "—oh, in ten minutes or so."

In his old life, Flint had been a partner in the ACT Legal Support Team, which provided skip-tracing, video and transcription services to law firms. Many of the business's clients had been high profile, Phelps Rendell being the most prestigious of the criminal attorneys. Flint's former partner, Terrence Clarke, had given her the man's name and number. Thankfully, Rendell had been understanding of the circumstances and thought highly enough of Flint to make a house call.

"If you won't do what's necessary to help yourself, Flint, then I will."

Either he would feel trapped and cooperate or walk out the door and not look back. Given his recent history, Nicky was counting on the first.

Holding her breath, she waited...

...and was relieved when Flint didn't budge from the couch.

PHELPS RENDELL arrived promptly at six-thirty. Flint noticed that, other than having earned more silver threads to grace his temples, the lawyer hadn't changed in the year and a half since they'd last worked on a case together. Barely forty, Phelps had reached a level of success that most criminal attorneys only dreamed about as reflected in his London-tailored suits and hand-sewn shirts.

If Nicky had to interfere, at least she'd secured the services of the best. Flint wasn't certain how he felt about it, though.

And so, the first thing he said to the lawyer was "I can't tell you when I'll be able to pay you," thinking that might scare him off.

Phelps merely arched a brow. "I haven't agreed to take the case yet." Then he shook Flint's hand. "Good to see you again, though the circumstances couldn't be worse."

"Worse is a relative term."

"Uh, can I get you some coffee?" Nicky interrupted.

"Thanks, nothing. I came directly from an early dinner meeting. What I'd like is to get right down to business."

Taking the seat opposite Flint, Phelps set his leather briefcase on the coffee table and pulled out both a microtape recorder and a lined tablet.

"Is it all right if I stay?" Nicky asked.

Phelps nodded. "I would prefer it. You may be of some help."

An understatement, Flint thought. Nicky would make certain she helped him, with or without his permission. When she'd made her announcement, he'd been tempted to leave. But something inside him responded to her caring. And he couldn't bring himself to insult her as he'd so obviously done by not letting her know that he was in trouble.

Phelps turned on the audio recorder and said, "Initial meeting with Flint Armstrong," then leaned back in his chair, pad of paper balanced on his crossed knee. "Start at the beginning. When did you meet Beverly Jensen?"

"A couple of years ago, through a case ACT was working on."

"Did you see her socially then?"

"We were both married to other people."

"That doesn't answer my question."

"No." He'd never cheated on Alana, despite her accusations, prompted, he was certain, by Cecilia. "Our relationship was strictly professional."

"When did that change?"

"Sometime before Thanksgiving." Weeks after he'd turned Scraps over to Nicky. "I ran into Beverly in a bookstore. We talked for a while over a cup of coffee."

"And..." Phelps was making notes to himself.

"Decided to have dinner later in the week."

"So you hit it off and started keeping company. Exclusive?"

"As far as I know."

"Would her seeing someone else have bothered you?" the lawyer asked.

"No. I wasn't in love with Beverly."

Flint couldn't miss the peculiar expression that suddenly crossed Nicky's features. Though she'd never objected, he'd had the feeling she hadn't approved of his being with another woman so soon after her sister's death.

"So tell me about Christmas Eve," Phelps continued.

That didn't take long. Flint repeated the story he'd given the police. About the party. His taking Beverly home. Waking up with her dead and his mind a blank.

"Apparently evidence showed signs of a struggle in the dining room. And they removed bits of carpet fibers from her nightgown."

Phelps asked, "Did they find your skin under her nails?"

"No."

"Did she have any cuts or bruises...other than the one that killed her?"

"A couple of bruises, I think." The past few days all blended together in his mind. "I didn't absorb it all."

"What about fluids?"

"Fluids?" Realizing what the lawyer meant—uncomfortable with Nicky listening—Flint cleared his throat. "Uh, no. Actually, I passed out before."

"Good. That's in your favor. The prosecution can't amend to a rape/murder charge with a more serious penalty. What about you?" Phelps asked. "Did they find any bruises? Muscle strain? Any evidence at all that you were involved in a struggle? Or that you might have dragged a deadweight and lifted it to your bed?''

Flint shrugged. "Beats me.''

"What are you getting at?'' Nicky asked.

"I'm just trying to determine how much physical evidence the prosecution has. Of course, I intend to follow up and get the all the details from official sources later.'' He turned to Flint. "What about similar incidents—''

"You mean have I ever been responsible for anyone else's death?'' Thinking of his late wife and child, Flint was unable to keep the irony from his tone.

"He means something weird happening while you were sleeping,'' Nicky said.

Flint told Phelps about his previous violent episodes while sleepwalking, and Nicky backed him up, citing Scraps as an eyewitness...as if a dog could take the stand.

"Committing violent acts while sound asleep.'' Phelps paused to scribble more notes on his pad. "Not an everyday occurrence, but I have heard of a few cases with similar circumstances. How long has this been going on?''

"It started when I was a kid...lasted for a year or so...and then not again until after the earthquake....''

Phelps nodded. "We'll need an expert opinion as to whether or not we can use this as a defense. I'll find out which is the best sleep disorder center in the area and get you scheduled in for evaluation. And I'll have the paperwork to release the crime scene drawn up.''

"You'll represent Flint, then?'' Nicky asked.

Her obvious excitement stirring Flint into feeling something like approval, as well.

"I'm not sure that any criminal attorney could pass up such an intriguing case," Phelps admitted. "I can't resist a new challenge myself."

"Flint is quite a challenge, all right," Nicky mumbled, turning a baleful eye on him.

Phelps wasted no time with small talk. He intended on playing catch-up immediately since the preliminary hearing was scheduled for the next morning. Assuring Flint that he'd meet him outside the courtroom, he took his leave.

When Flint turned from the door, Nicky was beaming with satisfaction. For a moment, he was caught by the flush of becoming color in her cheeks and the sparkle in her big blue eyes. He hadn't seen her look so happy for far too long.

Oddly enough, he, too, was feeling...well, something, anyway. Hard to put a name to what had become a foreign concept. He only knew his world seemed a slightly lighter shade of gray.

And so he was surprised when Nicky said, "You look tired. If you want to sleep...or just have some privacy...you know where to find the office cum guest room. Make yourself at home."

He would, but not yet. There was something he had to do first. Glancing at his watch, he noted it was barely seven-thirty.

"Good," he murmured. "That gives me plenty of time."

"Time for what?"

He tried to be evasive. "I need to go out for a while. I promise I'll be back...though you'd better give me a spare key if you have one."

Eyes wide, Nicky appeared alarmed. "Can I ask where you're off to?"

He thought to fib lest she try to stop him from leaving, but he couldn't. Not when Nicky had always been straight with him.

"According to the newspaper," Flint told her, "Beverly's wake is tonight." He watched her jaw drop when he announced, "And I plan to pay my last respects."

Chapter Three

Against her better judgment, Nicky insisted on going to the wake with Flint. She hadn't even considered trying to stop him, had figured that his being roused enough to insist on doing *something* was a positive sign.

They decided to use her car rather than walk the two blocks to fetch his. Nicky didn't object when Flint took the keys from her, insisting he drive. She understood his need to feel in control.

"Beverly is at the Eggers Funeral Home on Belmont," he told her, opening the passenger door.

She slid inside. "I know the place."

He'd taken her intrusion well enough, perhaps had welcomed it. He hadn't even complained about waiting an extra ten minutes while she'd changed into a dark cranberry skirt and sweater outfit suitable for a solemn occasion.

They'd only gone a quarter of a mile when Flint asked, "Are you sure you want to do this?"

On a scale of one to ten, *this* scored a zero. Not that she would admit as much.

Choosing to be evasive, she said, "I did know Beverly, if not very well."

Logic he accepted without further question.

Flint's need for a support system was the only reason she hadn't stayed home to devour a new murder mystery that a friend had given her for Christmas. Not looking forward to what was sure to be an unpleasant situation at best, she pictured them walking straight into a hornet's nest. After all, Flint had been charged with Beverly's murder. She couldn't imagine the dead woman's family welcoming him with open arms.

In her heart, she admired Flint's decision to pay his last respects to Beverly Jensen, no matter the reaction his presence might provoke. He really was an honorable man, and—contrary to his recent behavior—courageous. He must have felt something for the woman he'd had a relationship with, even if he hadn't loved her.

Nicky was still trying to overlook her own reaction at hearing him say so. That her heart had all but stopped—after which her pulse had raced like mad—had thrown her for a loop.

Perhaps that was the reason she had unusually little to say during the ten-minute ride to the funeral home.

Cruising by, Flint noted, "Parking lot's full."

As was the sidewalk in front of the building.

"People obviously held Beverly in high regard."

"True. But tragedy also attracts curiosity seekers. And reporters."

She remembered her sister and niece's funeral all too well. So many people no one knew; members of the press recording what should have been private moments. Nicky figured Flint was drawing on the same experience until she caught a glimpse of a newscam team on the corner. The television reporter was interviewing a fair-haired man who appeared to be consumed with as much anger as grief.

"Isn't anything sacred?" she murmured.

"Not when a buck can be made off someone's misery."

After parking on the next block, they remained on the opposite side of the street until they were directly across from the funeral home entrance, thereby neatly avoiding the television news unit. Nicky had no doubts that any reporters present would recognize Flint.

Thankfully, the short hike in the brisk night air had invigorated her, had allowed her to pull herself together, so she could be strong for Flint in case he fell apart.

But the stir they caused upon approaching the entrance seemed to energize him. With each step, he grew taller, his spine stiffer. If he noticed the shocked expressions or heard the angry murmurs around them, he didn't give the spectators the satisfaction of his appearing intimidated.

"Hey, that's Flint Armstrong!" a man shouted.

"Who's the woman?" another demanded.

"Looks like he already found himself a new companion."

Outraged that anyone would try to turn their being together into something questionable, Nicky glanced over her shoulder, intending to blister the idiot with a few choice words. That was when Flint wrapped a protective arm around her shoulders, and crushing her to his side, rushed toward the door. A series of flashes blinded her.

"Mr. Armstrong—"

"Miss, wait!"

Cast into a sea of people in the foyer, Nicky tried

covering her reaction to Flint's holding her so close. "Idiots," she grumbled in a low voice. "You should have given me the chance to tell them off."

His mien grim, Flint let go of her. "I should have known better than to bring you with me. You need a tough skin to deal with reporters."

"Are you trying to say you think I'm the delicate type?" she joked.

"Actually, yes."

Flint's sincere answer flustered her anew. But even if she hadn't accompanied him tonight, Nicky figured some newshound overeager for a story was bound to come after her sometime.

Uncomfortably aware of the sudden silence—and all eyes turning toward them—she refrained from arguing. Among those paying their last respects were a couple of uniformed policemen. Undoubtedly the place was loaded with cops and lawyers, considering Beverly had been an assistant state's attorney.

"Uh, maybe we'd better go in," she murmured.

Before someone threw them out.

Nodding, Flint took a deep breath and plunged forward, parting the crowd of mourners, many of whom continued to stare in shocked silence. Growing edgier by the moment, Nicky remained at his side until they were in the parlor where Beverly Jensen was laid out.

Then she backed off and let Flint do what he had to.

WALKING RIGHT UP to the casket gave Flint one of the most difficult moments in his experience...and he'd had plenty of those in the past year.

Not that he was bothered by the negative emotions

emanating from the countless shadowy and faceless people he passed. To *them* he paid no mind.

Hands clammy, Flint folded one over the other in front of him, stared down at the still woman shrouded in gray silk and faced his own culpability in placing her in that coffin. Her dark cloud of hair softly haloing her face, Beverly appeared as peaceful and lovely as she had the night he'd awakened to find her dead in his bed.

She really could be sleeping, he thought.

Dreaming...

He closed his eyes.

Thinking about Beverly's head lolling to the side like a broken doll's hurled Flint back to Christmas Eve. As he concentrated on summoning the event that led to her death, his pulse picked up and his breathing grew shallow. And for a second, Beverly was suddenly transformed into Alana, the crystal-clear image confusing him.

Frustrated, he pushed Alana away. Back to Beverly. Back to the moment that he'd realized she was dead.

But how had she died?

No matter that he willed himself to face the truth, he simply couldn't remember what had come before.

Image vanishing as easily as he'd recalled it, Flint conceded defeat and gazed down at his latest handiwork. First Alana. Now Beverly.

Was every woman who cared for him doomed to an early grave?

Beverly should have meant more to him. He'd *wanted* her to mean more. He'd needed respite from his loneliness and guilt and had thought a comfortable relationship might be the answer. Trying to get over her own divorce, Beverly had been willing to take him, flawed as he was. But a man couldn't dictate to his heart. While he'd cared for Beverly as a close friend, he hadn't fallen in love—as he'd recognized was happening to her.

So why couldn't he have broken off the relationship cleanly as he'd meant to do?

Why hadn't he rediscovered the internal strength that had once been second nature to him?

If he had, Beverly would have been out of his life before Christmas Eve. She would be alive now, rather than fated to rot away in some damn coffin.

"I'm so sorry, Beverly," he said softly.

"Sorry doesn't cut it," came an anguished voice to his right. "Sorry won't bring my baby back."

He turned to face Beverly's mother, Hannah Westcott, who was flanked by her surviving children, Susan and Jonathan. They clung to each other for support and, united, shrouded him with their hatred.

"Mrs. Westcott."

Knowing a gesture of friendship wouldn't be welcome, Flint white-knuckled his fingers together.

"How dare you violate our grief like this?" Mrs. Westcott demanded, her voice breaking. "W-wasn't taking Beverly from us e-enough?"

"I never meant to hurt her."

"Is that your defense? You didn't *mean* to?" Her eyes welled with renewed tears, and her voice rose as she repeated, "You d-didn't *mean* to?"

Susan put her arms around her sobbing mother. "He's not worth getting yourself sick over." She motioned to her younger brother. "Jonathan, take her someplace where she can get off her feet for a while."

"C'mon, Mom." The slender young man glared at Flint before leading his mother toward a seating area.

Though Susan's eyes were red-rimmed, they remained dry as she stared at him coldly. "I'd rather you left on your own, but if you refuse—"

"I'll go now," Flint assured her.

He'd paid his respects. He'd done his best to face the awful truth. There was nothing else here for him. Nothing he could make better.

He turned to leave...and walked straight into a closed fist.

A smack of pain below his left cheek jerked his head back, and he flew into the coffin, his shoulder whacking a spray of roses across the polished surface. The instinct to lay into the bastard surged through his blood, but considering where he was—and why he was there—Flint fought the impulse. He straightened, muscles fraught with tension, and held himself in check. He wouldn't dishonor Beverly by engaging in a brawl with her ex-husband, whose classic features had gone slack from too much booze.

None too steady on his feet, Eric Jensen yelled, "Fight me, you bastard!"

"This is neither the time nor the place, Jensen."

Restless spectators gathered round, their muttering to each other in irate tones egging the man on. Jensen grabbed Flint's jacket front and took aim again, obviously intending to deliver a second punch.

Flint would have let him.

But Susan grabbed the man's raised arm before he could do more damage. "Eric, please, stop this. *Now*."

Jensen shrugged off his sister-in-law's hand, then lowered his arm. His gaze burned into Flint's face as did the alcohol fumes, when he declared, "You'll regret stealing my wife from me, Armstrong!"

Knowing the reason for the divorce, Flint had no

pity for the grieving man. "Beverly divorced you before I was ever in the picture."

"She would have come back to me...but now she can't...all your fault! The only woman I'll ever love is dead and about to be buried, and you're walking around a free man. Well, not for long...not if I have anything to say about it!"

Flint would have liked to set the man straight, but that would only have prolonged the ugly scene. "I apologize, Susan," he said, backing off.

Suddenly aware of Nicky at his side, pale-faced and trembling, he regretted her being there to see this. He should have known something would happen to upset her, should have kept his plans to himself.

"Are you all right?" she asked, her concern for him as usual.

"I will be once we get out of here."

He turned to go and she with him.

Jensen's raised voice followed. "I'll see you in hell, Armstrong, if it's the last thing I ever do!"

NICKY KEPT her own counsel as they ducked out of the funeral home through a rear exit. The alley provided them with a reporter-free escape hatch. Thankful for small favors, she waited until they were in the car and on their way home before bringing up the topic of Eric Jensen.

"Beverly's ex was being interviewed by the newscam team when we arrived." The tall, good-looking fair-haired man who'd seemed so angry, she remembered. "Do you think whatever he said will make it to the air?"

"What does it matter?"

Nicky chose not to voice her fear that Eric Jensen's

accusations could prejudice Flint's case. She was already walking a tightrope to get his cooperation.

Instead, she asked, "Was Jensen straight about Beverly considering a reconciliation with him?"

"Not unless she'd lost her mind. Her loving husband abused her."

"Physically?"

"Only when he drank too much," Flint said with disgust. "Beverly admitted she kept making excuses for him until he put her in the hospital."

Nicky shuddered. She couldn't imagine any woman staying with a man who hit her, not even for a short while. "Did she prosecute, I hope?"

"She divorced him instead. Not that he left her alone. The bastard was so obsessed and jealous, he would show up unexpectedly and harass her, especially if she dared to see another man. He was making her life hell, so she got a restraining order against him."

"That was before the two of you got together?"

"Right. The first time Jensen followed us, he kept a legal distance. The next time, he was waiting for Beverly when I took her home." Flint's visage darkened. "He forced his way inside her town house and roughed her up some."

"And?"

"She finally had him arrested."

"But he's walking the streets like a free man, too," Nicky said thoughtfully, then caught her breath at the next idea that occurred to her. "Flint, how far do you think an obsessed man would go?"

Taking his eyes off the road for a moment, Flint glanced at her. "What are you getting at?"

"Hurting Beverly didn't bring her back." Only a

sick mind could think so. Jensen was definitely off the trolley there. "What if her ex-husband decided that, if he couldn't have her, no man could." She tested the idea that was taking firm root in her mind. "What if he murdered her?"

"Murder? Now you're reaching."

"Probably...but what if I'm not?"

"I'd give anything to know that I wasn't the one responsible for Beverly's death, but let's face facts, Nicky. She and I were the only people in the house that night."

"As far as you know."

"If the police found evidence of a break-in, they would have said so."

"If they even looked for one," she countered, wishing like everything they could get into his place to take a good look themselves. "You were the obvious suspect, Flint, so how hard do you think they tried to find evidence that would point to someone else? Eric Jensen could have picked a lock or discovered an unlatched basement window—"

"Possible but unlikely."

"—neither of which would be apparent unless the investigation was thorough," she continued. "And the *possible* part is what's important." She was desperate to find an alternative to Flint's being responsible for Beverly's death. And, once she got an idea into her head, she couldn't let it go. Her father used to say she could be as stubborn as a bulldog. "Besides, who knows what evidence the technicians might have found that didn't get into the official case report."

"Now you've got the authorities suppressing evidence?" Sounding impatient with her, Flint demanded, "To what end?"

"An easy resolution. Clearing a murder off the books."

"Beverly was one of their own. If they suspected murder...other than by *my* hand, that is...do you really believe they'd take the easy way out just to lighten the caseload?"

Nicky shifted in her seat. Flint had a point.

As an assistant state's attorney, Beverly Jensen had been part of an elite group. Her professional purpose was the same as that of the police—they'd worked hand-in-glove to bring criminals to justice. Members of the investigating team might even have known her. Therefore, her fate probably warranted even more careful attention than that of some ordinary Jane Q. Citizen.

"Well...I don't think the police would do anything but their best," she finally admitted, "but—"

"So drop it!"

Flint's tone was so brusque that it immediately set Nicky on edge. They were sitting at a red light. She glared daggers at him until he faced her.

"Why should I?" she asked more calmly than she was feeling. Perhaps he had good reason....

"Because I say so."

She started. "You're not the boss of me!"

"Nor you of me."

Something indefinable ignited between them like a spark along a live wire. Nicky's pulse raced and heat rose up her neck to her face. And then the light changed and Flint broke the connection.

Hunkering down in her seat to camouflage her reaction, she couldn't help but be defensive. "I haven't been telling you what to do."

"You've been trying to run my life."

"I certainly have not!" She'd merely been making certain he was all right. As a matter of fact, since he'd begun seeing Beverly, she'd done her damnedest to stay out of Flint's way.

"I had enough of that with Cecilia."

Nicky gaped. "You're accusing me of being like my mother?"

"If the shoe fits..."

"How, pray tell, am I controlling?"

"You bail me out of jail without so much as asking me if that's what I wanted. Then you decide I'm staying at your place. And let's not forget your contacting a lawyer to take my case without getting my permission."

Her temper flared. Comparing her to her mother. Of all the ingrates! She'd only been trying to help him.

"Well, I'm on a roll then, aren't I?" Not about to pass up any chance to prove he didn't commit some heinous crime no matter how angry he'd made her, she dug in her heels. "And you can't stop me from giving Eric Jensen a closer look."

When Flint suddenly stomped on the brakes, Nicky feared he would try to force her to cease and desist. She geared herself up for an escalation of their argument...until she realized they'd pulled up in front of her apartment and he was merely parking the car.

ROUNDING THE ESCORT, Flint held out the key ring. Nicky grabbed it from his hand, then stalked toward the building entrance while he brought up the rear.

If her back were any stiffer...he swore she'd grown a few inches.

"If you really want to go to some fleabag motel rather than stay here, don't let me stop you," she muttered as she unlocked the downstairs foyer door. "Never let it be said I'm anything like my mother."

What was left of his temper deflated. "Maybe I was overstating my case. I appreciate your giving me a place to stay."

"Fine."

Her spine softened a bit, but he could tell she was smarting. He wasn't really resentful of Nicky's trying to help him. Rather he was worried that she might get carried away. He didn't want her getting in deeper and deeper...and to what end?

So that, when all was said and done, she would feel like a fool for believing in him?

Following her up the stairs, Flint knew he would have to dissuade her from pursuing Eric Jensen...only not tonight. The morning would be soon enough. Surely then, when he was rested, he would come up with a convincing argument to let it alone. Even thinking about Nicky's tangling with Jensen made Flint uneasy. The bastard had harassed and battered Beverly despite the divorce.

Despite the restraining order.

What made Nicky think the man would hesitate to hurt her if she got in his way?

A weird feeling came over him. Should Jensen lay a hand on Nicky, he would...what?

Flint didn't have a clue. By the time Nicky opened her door, all the purpose he'd been feeling washed right out of him, leaving him running on empty.

Scraps waited for them directly inside. He danced from one human to another for attention.

Flint was patting him on the side when Nicky said, "Leash," and the dog flew to obey.

"Want me to walk him again?"

Her expression blank, she said, "Heaven forbid I should tell you what to do."

And Flint knew his best move was to bite his tongue and leave her alone. He was exhausted, anyway. What he needed more than anything was a good night's sleep....

As Nicky clipped the leash to the dog's collar, he reminded her, "Be sure to lock your door tonight."

She gave him an odd look. "I'll even push a dresser in front of it."

Flint nodded, satisfied that she would be safe for now.

One day at a time...he had trouble thinking any further into the future.

THE BED TWISTING and turning forced him from sleep. The earth was shifting...rumbling...screaming.

Those were human voices...

Outside, transformers popped. Inside, the electrical blue glow showed he was alone.

Objects toppled from their perches to smash against walls and floor.

Earthquake...

"Alana! Megan!"

He was flying from the bed. Dropping into a dark netherland as the building began to collapse in slow motion. He couldn't let anything stop him from getting to his wife and daughter. As the walls folded around him, he blindly chanced the moving rubble, shouting their names in desperation.

And to no avail.

Tremors receding, the earth suddenly went motionless. Hesitating, he felt as if his heart was pounding

*out of his chest. And then he struggled on until his
foot made contact with something soft.*

A body.

Alana...open eyes staring at him...

*Down on his knees, he shook her, gently at first,
and then harder, as if force could awaken her.*

*He tried concentrating only on her but eventually
had to face another fear. Had to look straight at
it...breach it. Only he was having a difficult time making his body cooperate. He could hardly move.*

*What had once been the door to his daughter's bed-
room hung twisted on its hinges, the black, endless
opening beyond luring him to further horror....*

A SHARP BARK startled Nicky awake.

"Scraps, what's up?"

Toenails clicked across the wooden floor before a
cold, wet dog nose pushed into her face. She squinted
at the bedside clock. Three a.m.

Groaning in protest, she said, "Don't tell me you
have to go out *now?*"

Scraps whistled through his nose and danced back
and forth between her and the door. His rising anxiety
quickly got through to her sleep-fuzzed brain. Even
knowing she would be chilled the moment her bare
feet met the floor, she hurled back the covers and
toughed it out. If the dog had to go, he had to go.
Time and circumstances didn't matter.

A cry from the depths of hell rooted her feet to the
floor, and the ensuing crash made her very blood run
cold. Scraps bumped her legs, setting her in motion.
He'd been trying to warn her....

Heart pumping like mad, Nicky ran to her unlocked
door and threw it open.

"Flint!"

Scraps squeezed by her and shot ahead. By the time she caught up to him, he was balanced on hind legs, front paws scrabbling at the guest room door. Nicky caught his collar and pulled him down.

"Easy, boy, easy. Shh."

Seeming to understand, the dog settled, anxious eyes glued to her face. Heart in her throat, Nicky wrapped her fingers around the doorknob, then experienced a moment's hesitation as another loud noise from inside made her wonder if entering would be safe.

But *Flint* was in there...not some monster.

Nerves taut, she hung on to the dog and turned the handle. The door creaked open and she peeked inside.

"Flint?"

Her eyes already adjusted to the dark, she could make out his form at the far end of the room. His movements erratic, he was feeling his way along her desk and bookshelf. A cry of frustration escaped him as if he couldn't find what he was searching for, and he threw himself against the wall next to the bed. Faint light from a curbside street lamp spilled through the nearest window and over his bent head and bowed bare shoulders. His expression was grim, musculature highly defined as if he were in the throes of a struggle.

And though his eyes were open and he was breathing hard, Nicky would have sworn he was either sound asleep or in some deep trancelike state.

Playing out some nightmare?

Nicky held her breath watching. Was this what had happened on Christmas Eve? *Had* Flint been out of control? Had he killed Beverly? Everything in her wanted to believe otherwise.

"Flint." Feet rooted in the doorway, she softly called out his name in the hopes of waking without startling him. "It's me, Nicky."

For a moment he remained frozen. Then a subtle change came over him. The tautness ebbed from his muscles and his features transformed. He ran a shaky hand through his hair and vented a low curse.

If he hadn't been awake before, he was now.

"Flint?" she repeated, letting go of the dog's collar.

Scraps took a few steps inside the room, sniffed the air, then, with a whine, trotted up to Flint and sat smack on his foot. Saying nothing, Flint reached down and absently patted the dog's head.

Nicky spotted the source of the crash that had alarmed her. A wooden chair lay off-kilter, one leg splintered. Pulse threading unevenly, she drew closer.

"Are you all right?"

Flint jerked away from Scraps, who continued to sit at alert. "The chair...I must have smashed it against the wall."

He sounded amazed...bewildered...and horrified.

The last grated on Nicky. An overreaction. It was only a chair, for heaven's sake. But she said nothing as Flint sank down on the edge of the bed and stared at his hands as if they'd betrayed him.

"You didn't hurt yourself, did you?" she asked.

He gazed up at her, his face twisted in agony. "I don't remember doing it, but I really must have."

And in the silence that followed, she knew it wasn't the chair he was thinking about at all, but Beverly. Without considering possible consequences, she moved closer to his side...and slid her arms around him in an instinctive gesture of comfort.

Only when her fingers touched his trembling back

did it register on her that he slept in the nude. Her thin cotton sleep shirt was all that separated her flesh from his. Breath catching in her throat, she froze.

Thought to pull away.

Too late.

Flint had already responded. He was wrapping his arms around her hips. The nightshirt slid up, exposing her naked bottom. Rather than chilling her, the cool night air swept over her flesh in a wave of unexpected sensuality. He pulled her so close that her knees smacked into the side of the mattress. Wedged between his naked thighs, she felt tortured, more so when he pressed his face into the softness of her belly...there smothering the sounds of his despair.

They were both in agony, if very different kinds.

Squeezing her eyes shut, Nicky bit back a moan and fought her imagination from going wild.

His flesh was warm...vibrant...damp with perspiration. Her flesh was becoming heated...tightening...yearning.

A big mistake. She shouldn't touch him so intimately. Not now. Not ever. He wasn't for her and never would be. Even knowing that, she threaded her fingers through Flint's dark hair, became mesmerized by the simple tactile pleasure, and held him so close they might as well have been one.

Her breasts and belly throbbed. Her chest hurt with every breath. A heat deep inside her, the likes of which she'd never before experienced, raged out of control. Every inch of her that touched him burned with forbidden fires.

Worse, painful emotions that she'd thought dead and buried years ago swamped her.

And Nicky knew she was in big trouble.

Chapter Four

Flint came out of the preliminary hearing wishing the judge had set his date with a jury of his peers sooner than the last week of January. A month seemed like forever when he just wanted to get it over with.

"I would have liked more time to prepare a case of this seriousness," Phelps was saying as they stopped in the lobby, "but it could have been worse. At least Dr. Galloway agreed to interview you immediately."

"Is that our sleep expert?" Nicky asked, blue eyes going wide. "You found one already?"

"I told you I was going to get on it right away," the lawyer reminded them. "I asked one of my medical experts for the name of a respected psychotherapist who specializes in sleep disorders. He knows Jane Galloway personally and made the contact. Dr. Galloway was intrigued. She called first thing this morning."

"So what's the drill?" Flint asked, not exactly amenable to having his psyche dissected.

"First you talk. Explain your history with these sleep disturbances. If Dr. Galloway thinks we have a defense, she'll schedule you into the clinic for physical tests that can prove you weren't responsible for your actions."

Flint tried to work up the appropriate enthusiasm, but he felt hollow inside.

Nicky quickly picked up the ball. "When do we...uh...when does Flint see her?"

Phelps checked his watch. "A little less than two hours. You have plenty of time for lunch."

"Great."

Phelps looked at *him* consideringly. "You could do with a more positive attitude, my friend."

"This is as positive as it gets."

The only thing Flint was positive about was being responsible for Beverly's death. And because of that, he was conflicted about a defense that might give him an acceptable excuse for murder.

"Work on him," Phelps told Nicky.

"I keep trying."

Wasn't that the truth!

Nicky had been persistently—if unnaturally—cheerful all morning, even after a disrupted night's sleep. How she was able to continue giving him such support, Flint didn't understand, not now that she had firsthand experience with his unpredictability.

Phelps left and Nicky excused herself for a quick trip to the rest room.

Flint waited to one side of the lobby. He leaned against a support column and let his mind drift back to the night before. Being capable of doing anything without conscience made him a sleepwalking sociopath.

As usual, he couldn't remember what had happened between his falling asleep and waking, though the broken chair obviously had been of his doing. Thank God he'd had the presence of mind earlier to warn Nicky to lock her bedroom door. Not that she'd had the good sense to stay put.

Fortunately, his streak of violence had played itself out before she'd found him. Who knew if she would be so lucky next time?

If there was a next time.

Flint was thinking that he should remove that possibility by removing himself from her apartment, when a gravelly voice jerked him back to his surroundings.

"Well, well, if it ain't Flint Armstrong."

Flint turned to face the familiar middle-aged man who stood three inches shorter and thirty pounds heavier than he did. "Shelton."

The man's dark eyes glittered with malice. "How does it feel to have the shoe on the other foot?"

Put off by the car parts dealer as much as ever, Flint glanced down at the floor. "Shoes are pretty comfortable, but thanks for your concern."

Sid Shelton barked a laugh, then protracted his full lips into a grimace, showing off capped teeth that were at least as expensive as the new suit stretched across his broad back. And Flint didn't remember seeing the Rolex before, either. Despite his legal entanglements, Shelton appeared to have a healthy cash flow.

"I wouldn't be so flippant if I were you, Armstrong," Shelton warned him. "With your pretty face and that fit physique, all the gang-bangers at Menard will be wantin' to sign your dance card."

The mention of the maximum-security prison infamous for being run by gangs set Flint's teeth on edge. Inmates who didn't sign up were subject to being used as sex slaves, cell mates trading their favors to other gang members for the price of a cigarette.

"What about you, Shelton?" Flint asked in a deceptively civil tone. "What are you doing here today? Bucking for an all-expenses-paid vacation? Or are you here to make another lottery payment to one of your victims?"

"You think you're so smart, don't you, Armstrong? I'm not the one knee-deep in horse manure this time." Shelton snickered. "Murdering an A.S.A.! I would've sworn you had more sense than that. They're gonna fry you, big man. I'd pay good money for a front-row seat."

"Hmm. Business must be better than ever."

Nicky's "Flint isn't going to fry" announced her swift return.

Aligned with him, she glared at Shelton, whose eyes widened as he checked her out from the tips of her spiked red hair to the toes of her boots.

"How can you be so sure, doll face?"

"Because Flint is innocent."

Shelton smirked. "So what? That and a buck-fifty'll get him on the bus."

He barked another laugh and retreated.

Flint stared after Shelton as he strutted toward the exit.

"Who *is* that unpleasant person?" Nicky asked. "And what does he have against you?"

"Name's Sid Shelton. He owns a string of car repair and parts shops. Not to mention a movable chop-shop operation. Terrence and I were partially responsible for his losing an expensive civil case with respect to that."

Now that Shelton had disappeared from view, Flint started across the lobby, guiding Nicky by the arm. He sensed she had a moment's discomfort at his touch, but when he glanced at her, she seemed fine. His imagination.

"If Shelton was dismantling stolen cars for parts...why a civil suit rather than a criminal prosecution?"

"Because he cut a deal with the State's Attorney's Office. He gave up information on a major car theft ring that was supplying him with the stolen vehicles." Flint held open the exit door, waiting for Nicky to pass through before following. "The speculation was that Shelton had gotten his own theft operation together and was willing to sell off the competition for immunity from prosecution."

"The authorities didn't even close him down?"

"Theoretically." Not that Flint believed men like Sid Shelton reformed. "In the meantime, one of his victims—someone with money to burn—decided to get justice where he could."

"The civil suit."

Flint nodded. "Which cleaned out Shelton's pockets of anything but spare change."

"Poverty has certainly given him an attitude," Nicky muttered.

"The attitude's nothing new. And chances are Shelton waited awhile and reopened his operation in a different location. My guess is the civil suit was merely an interruption of his cash flow. He doesn't exactly look needy."

They'd arrived at her car. Getting in, Nicky grew unnaturally silent, making Flint wonder what was buzzing around in that brain of hers. Whatever she was thinking, she kept it to herself. For once, Flint wished she would spit it out...say what was on her mind...anything so that he didn't have time to wonder how far inside *his* head Dr. Jane Galloway would be eager to probe.

His newest misadventure had left him with another haunting image—one he chose not to examine too closely.

One he certainly wasn't willing to share.

He was relieved when they arrived at a popular serve-yourself soup and sandwich joint several blocks from Lakeshore Medical Center, the near north facility that housed the Sleep Disorder Clinic.

Once they were ensconced in a booth, Nicky practically attacked her "bowl" of sourdough bread, scooped out in the middle and filled with hearty Southwestern chicken chili. Flint ignored her attempts to convince him to eat. He was getting so wound up about his coming appointment that he could hardly force down a cup of coffee.

As though she could read his mind, Nicky said, "I have a good feeling about Dr. Galloway."

Flint wouldn't openly admit to his dreading the session. "You always look at the bright side of things." Something he vaguely remembered having once been able to do.

"I figure life pulls us down too often as it is, so why cooperate?"

"We don't always have a choice."

"True." Having finished her chili, she was ripping the loaf of sourdough into edible chunks. "Though we can also find a way to pick ourselves up and start over."

He knew she meant him...the way he'd been since the earthquake. She'd rarely been direct about it, undoubtedly because he'd tended to shut her out.

"Sometimes it's too damn tough to find the psychic energy."

"Whoever said doing anything worthwhile was easy?"

Not wanting to continue in this vein, Flint grabbed a chunk of bread and stuck it in Nicky's mouth to shut her up. She made a funny face at him and chewed.

Watching her, Flint nearly smiled...and felt an unfamiliar tightening of his chest....

After inhaling every last crumb of her sourdough soup bowl, Nicky suggested they stretch their legs to get to the clinic rather than move the car.

"I can use the exercise," she said. "I missed my run this morning."

Because of him, Flint knew, remembering how she'd held him in her arms the night before until he'd dozed. "A walk would be good."

As they started off, he wondered how long she'd stayed before slipping away, presumably to her own room. When he'd stirred from a fitful slumber sometime after four, he'd been left with a half-empty bed and an even emptier feeling.

Odd as it seemed to him, he'd wished Nicky had stayed with him until morning.

Reclaiming sleep hadn't come easy. Then he'd awakened to the smell of kick-ass coffee just before six only to learn that Nicky had already been to his car. So that he'd have something fresh to wear to court, she'd retrieved the clothing he'd been carrying in his trunk—a fast change left from the week before when he'd gone to a holiday fund-raiser with Beverly directly after work.

He was assuming Nicky had gotten less sleep than he had. Not that anyone could tell by looking at her.

Below the velvet and satin hat she'd scrunched to the middle of her forehead, her cheeks were glowing. And as they headed east along a stretch of eateries, boutiques and banks, he noticed she hadn't lost the bounce to her step.

"I've been doing some more thinking about Eric Jensen," she said, her tone both reasonable and cautious. "I'm convinced we ought to give Beverly's ex-husband a good look."

"I thought we'd settled that issue last night."

"We did. Only we came to two different conclusions, remember?"

"I haven't changed my mind."

"Neither have I." Nicky held his gaze. "You might be willing to sit back on your butt and twiddle your thumbs while someone else decides your fate, but I'm going to be doing some digging on my own."

Flint might have let it go if he didn't have a gut feeling about Jensen. The man had a violent streak, whether or not he'd been drinking. Nicky getting in his face was bound to set him off. What Flint thought of as brotherly instincts went on alert. Besides, if she got hurt because of him…

"Stay out of this, Nicky, please."

"Don't start."

Thinking he could placate her while getting his way, he changed tactics. "There's no need for you to do anything on your own."

Her eyebrows shot up. "You want to clarify that?"

"Phelps Rendell is very thorough—it's the secret to his success. Leave things to him. If there's anything to find on Jensen, his investigators will get it."

Nicky did a lousy job at hiding her disappointment.

A frown pulled her eyebrows together and turned down the corners of her normally smiling mouth.

"You used to do some of that investigating for him yourself," she said.

"I'm not in the business anymore."

"This *is* your business, Flint."

"So why don't you keep that in mind?"

"I am."

She was impossible. "Did you share your suspicions with Phelps?"

"When did I get the chance?"

"Then I guess that's your next step."

"I'll tell him about Eric Jensen," she conceded. "But the more people out looking for answers, the more likely we are to find them."

"The answer is right in front of your nose."

Nicky said, "Maybe," though she didn't look convinced. "But don't you want to get rid of any doubts? Do you really want to go the rest of your life not knowing for certain? Do you really want to carry around another load of guilt when maybe it doesn't belong to you?"

Her intensity got to him.

Why was his state of mind—and his fate—so important to her?

Her concern and actions went beyond those of the typical in-law. Then, again, Nicky wasn't a typical anything. She was special and he'd always cared for her as much as he would a real sister. He guessed she considered him family, too, despite Alana's death.

Certain she wouldn't listen to reason about Eric Jensen, Flint grew edgy. No matter how hard he tried to persuade or coerce her, she would steam ahead until she got herself into trouble.

He couldn't have that.

So, for her sake, he said, "You're right. I do want to know."

"Great." She beamed as if she'd been struck by a ray of sunshine. "And while we're at it, we should check on anyone else who might have had reason to want Beverly dead. As an assistant state's attorney, she had to have made plenty of enemies putting the bad guys away...not to mention any enemies *you* might have made by supplying law firms with incriminating information."

Why wasn't he surprised? "Enemies like Sid Shelton, I suppose?"

"He said he'd *pay* to see your execution," Nicky reminded him. "What if he got into your house intending to kill *you,* but ran into Beverly instead?"

Once she was on a roll...

But Flint didn't object no matter how crazy this sounded to him. Let her get carried away if that would make her happy. He suddenly realized he *wanted* to make her happy. Putting a smile on Nicky's lips made him feel more at peace with himself.

So they'd be wasting their time. Big deal. What else did he have to do until he was locked away for good...if not worse?

Shelton's comment about paying to see him fry did rankle.

At least Nicky could keep his mind occupied with other things.

And he could keep her safe.

NICKY STEWED all the way home when Flint wouldn't let her wait for him at the clinic.

Why not?

Because he hadn't known how long it would take—as was his excuse—or because he was tired of her company?

Though she'd wanted to push for the real reason, she'd had the good sense to back off. He needed space. He'd gotten used to a solitary existence, answering to no one. Pressure of any kind seemed either to incapacitate him or to get his back up as he had with her. She hadn't forgotten how he'd accused her of being like her mother.

Continuing to be disgruntled by the comparison as she parked the car at the end of her block, she stopped cold when she spotted her mother leaving her building.

What now?

Nicky was sorely tempted to hide behind some evergreen bushes, but then she'd have to pretend she hadn't known about Cecilia's attempted visit, and she'd never been good at lying. Nicky sighed. The best she could do was put on a fake smile and face the music. She had no doubts her mother's snit, obvious even from a distance, concerned Flint.

"Hey, Mom!" She kept her tone light as she rushed toward her mother. "What's up?"

Cecilia Keating stopped in her tracks halfway to the curb. "That's what I want to know."

Catching up to her, Nicky kissed her cheek. "What? A girl can't even leave her apartment without explanations?"

Her mother whipped a tabloid newspaper from under her arm and displayed the front page directly under Nicky's nose. "Explain this!"

Nicky's eyes nearly popped out when she saw the picture of her and Flint that had been taken as they'd entered the funeral home. She knew he'd placed his arm around her and had pulled her close to shield her from the media, but the photograph looked so...so intimate.

The headline was worse: Accused Replaces Murdered Lover.

"Now I'm *really* ticked that I didn't chew out those reporters," she muttered.

"Nicole!"

Oh, boy.

A movement from the interior of a strange car parked across the street caught her attention. She could make out no more than the blur of a pale face turned their way. Someone was watching them! Obviously one of those overeager newshounds had tracked her down. Nicky was tempted to march right over to the Buick and tell him or her off...but now wasn't the time for a confrontation.

Instead, she took her mother's arm and spun the woman back toward the building's entrance. "Come on inside and I'll make you something warm and soothing to drink."

Definitely something without caffeine.

Thankfully, her mother didn't swing into an immediate diatribe. Truth be told, she was unusually reticent.

Once upstairs, Nicky put on the kettle, then ran Scraps out the back way for a quick look at the alley. By the time she served the herbal tea that promised a calming effect, she'd pulled herself together.

Not so her mother.

Her expression that of one betrayed, Cecilia took only a tiny sip of tea from her mug before asking, "Nicole, how could you?"

"Go to the wake? I did know Beverly Jensen." Nicky hedged as she had with Flint.

"I meant how could you get yourself so involved with that man."

Nicky sighed. Would her mother ever say the name *Flint* again?

"We already went over this yesterday morning," she reminded her.

"Only about your visiting him to offer your support." Cecilia tapped the newspaper with a perfectly manicured nail. "According to this article, you bailed him out!"

"Someone had to."

"Why couldn't you let him stay behind bars?"

Nicky's hand tightened around her mug. "Flint doesn't belong in a jail cell."

"And where *does* he belong, Nicole?"

"In his own home."

"Which he cannot yet enter," her mother informed her. "Before I came here, I drove by the house for a look. All those ghastly yellow tapes pointing it out as a crime scene...and both doors are padlocked."

Which sounded like more than a quick look. "Flint's lawyer is working on that."

"And in the meantime?" Her mother's gaze slid toward the bedroom doors.

If ever Nicky wished she could lie with ease, this was the time. Instead, she admitted, "Flint is using my office for a few days."

Cecilia fell back onto the couch cushions in what Nicky could only describe as a half-swoon. She wondered if her mother had perfected the technique as part of her stage act. Three decades before, as Cecilia Lawrence, she'd made a meager living singing in lounges—dives, Nicky's father had called them, although her parents had met in one.

"You'll be the death of me yet," her mother gasped, hand to her chest.

"There's nothing wrong with your heart," Nicky returned, disturbed by the aura of melodrama. Maybe if her mother's eyes weren't filled with unshed tears that looked all too real, she would be able to shrug it off. "And you're the strongest woman I know."

Strongest willed, anyway.

"Are you having an affair with him?"

"Affair?" Nicky's pulse did a jig even as she protested, "Mom, Flint was my sister's husband. I said he was staying in my office, not in my bedroom."

That she'd held him for nearly an hour in the narrow bed the night before was none of her mother's business. Nor was her torturing herself over him throughout the early-morning hours afterward. She only hoped her mother wasn't perceptive enough to see through her fudging.

"Thank heavens he doesn't have that strong a grip over you."

Nicky squirmed in her chair. "Flint's no Mesmer. And I doubt I could be hypnotized anyway." At least not into doing something she was dead set against.

Her mother picked up her mug and took a healthy draft of tea before saying, "Nicole, promise me something."

All her nerve endings went on alert. How often had her mother coerced Alana into doing what she wanted after using that same preamble?

"You know I never make promises without first hearing the whole deal."

"I only want you to be careful around him," her

mother said, still avoiding saying Flint's name. "I don't know what I'd do if anything bad happened to you."

Nicky took a deep breath. She didn't want anything bad happening, either. Not to anyone.

"Sure, Mom. I promise I'll be careful." And, trying to turn the tables on her highly emotional parent and get some information she'd been wanting, Nicky added, "I hope you're being careful, too."

"Me? Whatever about?"

"The new man you've been dating. What did you say his name was?"

Her mother started. "I don't believe I did."

"You're right." Why not? "Why so secretive?"

"You're imagining things."

"Not telling your own daughter who you're seeing is imagining things?"

"Oh, heavens, his name is Oren Maticek."

Her mother couldn't hide the pleasurable smile that curled the edges of her mouth. Nicky smiled, too.

"Oren. Nice, solid name. So tell me about him."

"Nothing to tell. Not yet." The twinkle in her mother's eyes changed into something far more serious when she said, "He has to prove himself first."

Because of her own father walking out on them? Nicky wondered. Her mother had always been attractive enough to other men, but none had stuck around for long.

Nicky chose not to press for more answers at the moment. Her mother had never been open with *her* concerning feelings about men. Nor about any of the simple inconsequential mother-daughter things she used to share with Alana. Nicky had so often felt left out. But all that was changing. She had to be patient.

Only when she was finally alone did Nicky question the significance of her taking Alana's place in her mother's affections. Did it mean Cecilia was turning to her naturally? Or that Nicky was pushing too hard, as Flint had accused her of doing?

"I'm not Alana," she told Scraps, who'd trotted into the room to keep her company. "I never wanted to be her."

Though she'd loved her older sister, she hadn't been blind to Alana's faults. Not that she didn't have a few of her own. She'd wanted some of what had come so easily to her sister, though, and now she seemed to be getting her wish.

Only at what cost?

Were her mother and Flint turning to her for those things that made her Nicky? Or did they merely see her as an Alana-substitute?

Staring down to the street, she realized the strange car was still there. A weird sensation crept up her spine as she thought about someone spying on her.

Nicky shook herself. No time for self-indulgence. This wasn't about her.

She had Flint to worry about.

Not to mention the possibility of there being a *real* murderer.

Chapter Five

"Natural disasters often trigger sleep disturbances in those who survive," Dr. Jane Galloway said after Flint told her about the earthquake reviving his childhood problem with a vengeance. "Especially if their loved ones don't."

Flint found himself responding to the compassion offered by the psychotherapist—an attractive, silver-haired woman whom he guessed to be in her mid-fifties. A reflection of her own sophisticated appearance, her office was anything but clinical. He felt as if he were a guest in a very inviting home rather than in a functional hospital room. They sat in opposite leather chairs, a lacquered table between them.

"I should have been able to save them," he told her.

"How?"

"If I hadn't been sleeping so soundly... Alana always laughed about my being able to sleep through an earthquake." Some joke.

"And you believe that you could have changed that tendency if you had somehow known what was going to happen?"

Emotionally, yes. But logically, practically...

"Probably not."

"Still, you feel responsible."

"I dragged my wife and child to California. Alana didn't want to go."

"Then why did she?"

"So I wouldn't leave her."

Flint had never admitted this to anyone. Telling a stranger was easier than someone he was close to. Like Nicky. Considering the strength of her loyalty, he could only imagine what Nicky would think if she knew he'd been ready to desert a sinking ship.

"How long were you and your wife having problems?"

"Practically from the day we married, although it took me years to realize how serious things had gotten. My wife's mother had what you might call undue influence over Alana. Cecilia Keating was the epitome of the stick-her-nose-in-everything mother-in-law. She was used to making Alana's decisions for her and wasn't about to give that up just because her daughter had a new husband."

"What kind of decisions?"

"Everything from where we should live to how we should spend our money."

"And your wife went along with this?"

"Looking back, I figure it was easier for Alana to defer to her mother rather than sharing these decisions with me. And then there was Alana's career, probably the most direct extension of her mother. Cecilia's singing went nowhere, so she lived vicariously through her more talented daughter. Alana didn't really care if she 'made it.' She loved music and really wanted to teach. But after Alana graduated from college with a degree in music education, Cecilia managed her into booking after booking...."

Not that he'd cared what his wife had worked at...if only it had been her decision...or at least if it had made her happy.

"So you blame your mother-in-law for the disintegration of your marriage."

"No, actually I don't. Cecilia was only the catalyst. I blame myself for not making a move sooner. I was too busy building a business to notice quite how much influence she continued to hold over Alana. I was pretty dense about the seriousness of the situation until after Megan was born."

He could hardly say his daughter's name without breaking up. Just knowing the light in her clear blue eyes had been snuffed out forever ate at him. Only by sheer will did he keep his composure.

"Take your time," Dr. Galloway said.

But he'd had enough time to think about how things had gone wrong.

"A child is supposed to bring a couple together. We grew further apart. Cecilia wanted to have priority with her grandchild, as well, and Alana was willing to allow it. At my insistence, we tried marriage counseling...." Remembering his frustration when Alana wouldn't shut her mother out, he shook his head. "Eventually I realized the only solution was to get my family as far away from here as I could."

"California."

"Exactly." Flint remembered the circumstances leading to the disaster. "I sold my share of the business to my partners and moved without having a job. Alana wouldn't agree to sell our house for a year in case things didn't work out." In case she changed her mind, he'd been certain. "That's why we were living in the apartment building that collapsed. I didn't think ahead. I didn't properly prepare...."

Flint wound down and waited for Dr. Galloway's reaction. Expression thoughtful, she was making copious notes. Then she looked up over her half glasses, insightful blue eyes boring into him.

"Let's see if I understand what you see as being your alternatives to what did happen." She tapped the tip of her forefinger. "You could have remained here in Chicago, which might have resulted in a divorce." A second finger. "You could have noticed how much your wife deferred to her mother earlier in the marriage and moved then." A third. "Or, at the very least, you could have planned the move better, so that you would have had a job first—that way, you could have been living in a house rather than in the apartment building that collapsed—even if that meant staying under your mother-in-law's influence longer."

"Correct," he said, though listening to her reiterate made him wonder if any had been a better solution. He shifted uneasily and went on the offensive. "Why are we dissecting my marriage rather than the violent episodes I can't control or remember?"

"I need to understand what brought you to that state. The intolerable stress before. The horror of the disaster itself. The overwhelming feelings of guilt after."

"I don't know what else I can tell you."

"You can tell me how you felt when the sleep-walking episodes began."

"Felt?" All he could recall was a void—a never-ending interior of mirrors that reflected nothing. "Empty," he said, realizing that was no longer exactly true. He recognized a subtle difference in himself. "Dead."

"Like your wife and child."

"I hope to God they're in a better place than I've been," he said past the lump in his throat.

Dr. Galloway busied herself skimming her notes, but Flint suspected she was giving him a moment to compose himself.

"Tell me," she said, meeting his gaze, "about the incidents themselves. From the beginning."

Flint told her what he could, which wasn't much, considering he never had any memory of his actions while asleep. He recounted less than a dozen episodes, the first having occurred about two months after the earthquake. He'd awakened in the living room, standing over a broken lamp. A few other times he'd merely found himself in some place other than his bed. Once he'd put his fist through the wall outside of Megan's bedroom. He'd had to pay a visit to the E.R. that time. And then there had been the incident with Scraps.

"Do you ever remember anything afterward?" Dr. Galloway asked.

"Nothing about what I did while sleepwalking."

"What, then?"

"It's like I'm having a flashback. A single image...a terrifying feeling. Usually I see Alana...trapped...lifeless."

"Anything else?"

His gut knotted. He'd been dead set against sharing the other, more horrific memory. "I can't..."

"Then don't. Not until you're ready," Dr. Galloway told him, again skimming through her notes. She gave him another moment before asking, "Has anyone ever been privy to your sleepwalking?"

Words touched with irony, he said, "Beverly Jensen...though she'd make an unreliable witness."

The barest flicker of wry humor crossed the psychotherapist's fine features. "Anyone else?"

Flint hated involving Nicky, but she would insist on it. When she met Dr. Galloway—which no doubt she would make it her business to do—she was bound to say something about last night. She'd be ticked off big-time if she learned he hadn't mentioned it. Worse, rather than accepting this as being his way of protecting her, she would feel hurt.

"My sister-in-law, Nicole Keating."

"When was this?"

"Last night."

"Only a few nights after Ms. Jensen's death."

"The sleepwalking is becoming more frequent." A fact that horrified him. "How do I know I won't hurt someone else?" Like Nicky herself, he thought, knowing that getting out of her life would be the safest thing for her. "How can I make these episodes stop?"

"Perhaps by working on what instigated them in the first place. Not the actual earthquake, of course, but the feelings of guilt you harbor."

He'd allowed all suggestions of professional counseling to drift into the void....

"You believe me, then? About Beverly?"

"Your story is plausible, Mr. Armstrong. Surviving a disaster is trauma enough to disturb anyone's normal sleep patterns. And your having had night terrors as a child predisposes you to similar incidents as an adult. The sleepwalking, breaking things, remembering only that single image—it all fits. Now we have to prove you have a sleep disorder clinically."

"How?"

"By your spending the night here, under surveillance. One of my patients had to cancel. Business is keeping her from making it back into town when she thought she would. Her bad luck is your good fortune," Dr. Galloway said with an encouraging smile. "We can begin tomorrow night."

Almost immediately.

Some of the weight lifted from Flint's soul.

Upon leaving the hospital, however, he had to ask himself why.

The clinical assessment would undoubtedly lead to Dr. Galloway's agreeing to testify in his behalf, Phelps would have the defense strategy that he was hoping for, and maybe he himself would be found innocent of murder—none of which would return the dead to life.

Flint began wandering aimlessly and found himself at the north end of Lincoln Park, a beehive of activity despite the winter weather.

Cross-country skiers shushed over the snowy fields, joggers bounced along the cleared paths, and skaters braved the North Pond despite the recorded warning blaring at them to stay off the unsafe ice.

By contrast, all their worldly possessions gathered in black plastic bags that filled shopping carts stolen from grocery store parking lots, several homeless people huddled together for warmth around a bonfire they'd started in a metal garbage container.

As unbelievable as it seemed, Flint could identify with them...or at least with the hopelessness of their situations.

And yet...

The homeless worked hard at keeping body and soul

together to survive. What had he been doing for himself?

Coasting.

Leaving his fate for others to decide.

Knowledge that suddenly shamed him.

Shoving gloved hands deep into his pockets, Flint took possession of an unoccupied bench, where he watched couples and families and groups of friends having fun together. As it had been doing for far too long, life passed him by...only now his mind wouldn't shut down.

Flint found he couldn't stop thinking about Nicky. She'd stood by him when he'd driven other friends away. Why? He wondered that she had any use for him at all. Or perhaps she just pitied him.

That thought rankled.

Pity was for the weak. And no matter how far he had sunk, he hadn't done so out of weakness, Flint knew, but from the depths of despair and guilt. Because his lack of caring for himself had ended the life of a woman who hadn't deserved to die, he had to do something about it. He couldn't let himself get so out of control again.

He couldn't endanger Nicky.

Dr. Galloway seemed to believe that, with help, he could work through the issues that motivated his night terrors. If he could stop himself from sleepwalking, he couldn't harm anyone else.

Perhaps he couldn't go back to having a real life, but he wouldn't deny one to another person if he could prevent it.

Small comfort, but the best he could hope for.

NICKY NEARLY WENT out of her mind wondering where Flint was. That she should have already heard from him struck her as the day grayed with the setting sun. Soon she was pacing, glancing out the window every few minutes. When she started trying to conjure him out of the darkness that crept over the slush-filled street, she knew she was overreacting.

After all, Flint Armstrong was a grown man. He didn't answer to her. He'd said so. Maybe he'd decided to bunk somewhere else for the night.

So why hadn't he called to tell her?

Ordering herself to find something to do other than worry, Nicky decided to make a few telephone calls of her own.

First she tried to contact Beverly's office, hoping someone would talk to her about the dead woman's ex-husband. Too late. A recorded voice informed her the offices were closed for the day. Leaving a message was out of the question. Besides, she didn't even know whom to ask for, and a surprise visit after doing a little research might be better anyway.

Next, she checked in with Phelps Rendell, who was interested in if not impressed by her suspicions of Eric Jensen. As Flint had told her, the lawyer was thorough. He agreed to have Beverly's ex-husband checked out, and for good measure, would find out why Sid Shelton had been in court that morning.

Finally, she called one of Flint's former partners. Terrence Clarke said he'd be more than willing to help in any way possible, and yes, they could come into the office first thing the next morning to access the company's computer.

But when Nicky hung up, and she still hadn't heard from Flint, she was wondering if she'd be exploring the Internet alone.

Wandering back to the window, she glanced down to the street and noticed the same strange car parked on the other side. Too dark to tell whether or not the interior of the fancy silver Buick was occupied. Undoubtedly not, Nicky assured herself. A reporter would have made his or her move by now or would have left. Undoubtedly her suspicions were unfounded—after all, she didn't know every vehicle in the neighborhood.

She was so intent on her speculations that the sound of the apartment door opening gave her a good start. She whirled around, heart pounding, to face Flint himself. Relieved that he'd returned—rather than disappearing into the night as she'd begun to fear—she tried to read him, to sense his mood. Though she picked up some odd vibes, Scraps didn't seem put off. The dog picked up one of his squeeze toys and trotted over to the man who was removing his jacket and hanging it on the coat tree.

"Hi." She stopped herself from questioning him about his recent whereabouts. He was here now. Safe. That was all that mattered. "How did it go?"

Patting the dog and playfully tugging at the toy, he said, "Dr. Galloway thinks we may have a case."

Nicky didn't realize how tense she'd been while waiting for the psychotherapist's initial judgment. "That's great." She took what felt like her first full breath since they'd parted company earlier.

"Phelps will be pleased."

But what about him? Nicky wondered, not hearing any emotion in Flint's voice.

Looking at him more carefully, she thought he seemed a bit stiff. A little removed. Surely something had to touch him. He couldn't go on acting like a robot. He was flesh and blood, for heaven's sake.

A real man, as she well knew.

Remembering how much of a man stirred Nicky instantly. She couldn't erase the sensations that had swamped her when she'd held his nude body against her. Paranoid that she was sending off signals—Flint was staring at her, his gray eyes glinting strangely— she thought to take the dog for an extra walk so she could cool down and pull herself together.

But before she could make her move, Flint said, "Nicky, we have to talk. I've been doing some serious thinking."

Uh-oh. She didn't like the sound of that.

He was pacing the length of the room, she realized, looking for all the world like a man with a purpose. She blinked. The sudden change in him was startling. This Flint reminded her of the one she used to know. The one who took charge of things.

Sinking into her chair, she asked, "What about?"

"I don't want you in danger because of me."

"That's not your decision. I told you I'd do some digging with or without you."

"Not that. I mean *me.*"

Certain of what was coming next, Nicky dug her fingers into the chair's arms so she wouldn't overreact. Then the telephone rudely interrupted, putting off whatever he meant to tell her. She stared at the instrument sitting on a side table.

After the phone rang a second time, Flint asked, "Aren't you going to answer it?"

"Yes, of course." Flying to her feet, she crossed to the table and picked up the receiver midway through a third ring. "Hello?"

For a moment, she thought the caller had been impatient and had already hung up. Then she realized the connection was still live.

"Hello? Who is this?"

Someone was breathing into the receiver.

Frowning, she said, "I know you're there...."

"*Who's* there?" Flint demanded, drawing closer.

Starting to get annoyed when the person on the other side refused to say a word, she said, "Probably some cowardly reporter."

Flint grabbed the receiver from her and yelled into it. "If I'm the one you're interested in, say what you have to say." A few seconds later, he lowered the phone. "Whoever it was hung up." Thoughtful, he asked, "What made you say a reporter was calling?"

"I take it you didn't see this morning's newspapers."

Nicky fetched the tabloid her mother had left behind and handed it to him. His visage immediately darkened and he swore under his breath.

"Great. They identified you."

Nicky shrugged. "Big deal." All the name-calling in the world couldn't hurt her if she didn't let it.

"Since your phone number is listed, you can expect more crank calls like that one."

"So I'll let the answering machine pick up and screen them."

"But that won't stop a hungry reporter from getting your address and camping on your doorstep," Flint said tightly.

"Actually, I already thought that..."

She told Flint about the Buick, but when they crossed to the window so she could point it out to him, the car was nowhere in sight.

"Gone. It must have belonged to a neighbor, after all," she said. "Or an innocent visitor." Which she hadn't even considered and would account for her never having seen the vehicle before.

"Or, since the car disappeared right after I arrived," Flint added from directly behind her, "someone who wanted to find out whether or not I was staying here."

She noticed he didn't say *reporter,* though she was certain that was what he'd meant. Flint was so convinced of his own guilt, he wouldn't entertain any more sinister possibilities. She knew he was going along with the Eric Jensen thing, not because he believed the man might have done in his ex-wife, but because he was worried about *her* safety.

A fact that warmed her all the way down to her toes.

Standing so close to him warmed her even more. But this was the same troubling awareness that she'd experienced the night before. Nicky tried to move, but her legs wouldn't cooperate. And Flint's intense expression as he gazed down into her face didn't help any, either.

Her pulse threaded unevenly and her breath caught in her throat. He looked for all the world like a man who was seeing her as a woman rather than a kid. Her mouth went dry. Was it possible?

Confusion filled her. He'd been married to her sister for nearly six years. That put him off-limits. Didn't it? Besides, she'd already decided that she didn't want to be a substitute for anyone.

Nicky was the first to drop her gaze. She moved away from Flint on knees of rubber.

Running a hand along the back of the couch, she asked, "So what were you going to tell me before the phone rang?'' As if she didn't know where he'd been headed. Maybe removing the temptation to forget who they both were would be best, so when he didn't immediately speak up, she prompted him. ''You were saying something about my being in danger from you.''

''Right. I think it would be best if I—''

''Left,'' she finished for him.

She wouldn't try to stop Flint, but neither would she give up on helping to clear him of the charges. After that, she would concentrate on her own life.

''I could leave...if that's what *you* want,'' he agreed, surprising Nicky.

She'd been so certain of what he'd been about to tell her. ''Not really. I'd rather you stayed.'' The truth, if not the wisest course of action.

''Good. I can't see abandoning you now that the wolves have picked up your scent.''

''A colorful way of putting things, but by comparing them to tabloid reporters, you're doing the wolves an injustice.'' Curious, she asked, ''What *did* you have in mind?''

His ''I want you to tie me to my bed tonight'' was the last thing she expected to hear.

''Excuse me?''

''A tried-and-true method for keeping sleepwalkers from hurting themselves...or anyone else.'' Flint's expression was perfectly serious. ''What do you say?''

''I can't say I'm into S and M,'' she admitted, unable to hold back a snicker. ''Do I have to wear black leather?''

His expression lightened and she thought he might even crack a smile.

"Dominatrix Nicky?" His gaze swept her diminutive height. "I don't think that'll work for you."

"Hey, don't count me out. After teaching physical education to inner-city teenagers for five and a half years, I'm as tough as they come."

She demonstrated with a couple of street-survival moves based on martial arts skills. Not only did Flint smile, he laughed outright. The sound infectious, Nicky stopped what she was doing and laughed with him.

Lightening the mood between them was exactly what they both needed, she realized. It made spending some downtime together easier. The next few hours were tension free.

Bedtime was a different story, however.

Having just come in from walking Scraps, they were in the process of removing their outer gear when Flint said, "I was serious about your tying me up."

Suddenly edgy, Nicky covered with a light, "Did you bring the rope?" and threw her jacket on the coat tree.

"Not exactly. I thought something a little easier on the wrists?"

He removed his shoes and set them by the front door.

Just like they belonged there.

"A torn bed sheet?" she joked.

He started undoing shirt buttons. "Silk scarves?"

"You'll have to settle for polyester."

"No problem."

Big problem.

All that banter about S and M earlier didn't go to waste. Once triggered, Nicky's imagination fired.

Ducking her head so Flint couldn't see her blush,

she muttered, "I'll go find something," and hurried off, Scraps on her heels.

Nicky wished she had thought to fetch some nice, safe bungee cords from the car while they were out. Safe as they might be, she wasn't about to brave the cold yet again.

Pillaging her accessory drawer, she came up with two scarves that would do. Definitely not silk. Both were serviceable cotton squares that she used to keep the sweat from dripping in her eyes during her daily runs in the summer.

She felt like running now....

Leaving her bedroom, she didn't see Flint, so she stopped outside his open door and averted her eyes.

"Are you decent?" she asked, her soft-spoken question competing with the beat of her heart.

"I'm not sure about decent, but I'm ready and waiting."

The answer shot extra adrenaline through her.

The bedside lamp was on the lowest setting. Expecting Flint would be naked under the covers, Nicky was relieved to find him dressed in a T-shirt and the pants he'd been wearing when she'd bailed him out of jail. Even so, tying him up was no impersonal task. She had to sit on the edge of the bed, her hip touching his, and try to ignore the sensual images that immediately crowded her mind.

As she wrapped the first piece of folded material around Flint's right wrist, Nicky thought about how vulnerable he would be with both hands secured.

She could do anything to him she liked....

"You'll have to do better than that," Flint said.

Mouth dry, she whispered, "What?"

Her fingers froze on his wrist. His pulse seemed to

jump out at her and race up her arms all the way to her breasts.

"Tighter. Or I'll be able to pull free."

"Oh. Much tighter and you won't have any circulation." Reminding herself to keep breathing, she adjusted the knot slightly. "Better?"

"It'll do."

Nicky secured the remaining material to a slat in the headboard. "Why both arms?" The more she tried to ignore the seductive warmth of his flesh as it met the pads of her fingertips, the more impossible the task. "Surely tying one down is enough to keep you in line."

She needed to get out of the room—fast—before she made a fool of herself.

"What if it isn't?"

"I'm willing to take that chance."

"I'm not," he said softly.

Flint held out his left arm. Nicky touched him, then hesitated, for a moment forgetting what he wanted of her before fumbling with the second scarf. Somehow she managed to wrap the material around his wrist.

"Make the knot tight enough," he reminded her.

When she'd done so, he lifted his arm to the headboard. She shifted on the mattress, reaching over him to secure the scarf to another slat. Her mistake. She should have circled to the other side of the bed. As it was, practically her whole body slid against his, the erotic movement flushing her with heat. She finished the job in a building haze of sensuality.

As she straightened, Nicky met Flint's gaze for the first time since entering the bedroom. She couldn't read him, not because he was closing himself off from her, but because he was confusing her. He wasn't looking at her in a brotherly fashion at all. His lips parted and he wet them with his tongue.

Tempting...oh, so tempting...

Coming to her senses, Nicky jumped off the bed. "If you need anything...yell."

"I hope not." Thick lashes shuttered the expression in his gray eyes from her. "We could both use a good night's sleep."

"Right."

Too bad she wouldn't be getting one.

Chapter Six

Flint followed a yawning Nicky into the downtown offices of ACT Legal Support Team—ACT standing for the partnership of Armstrong, Clarke and Torres—trying not to imagine what life would be like if he'd never sold his share of the company and moved to California.

Talking to the receptionist who'd been hired since he'd left the year before, Linda Torres looked up at the sound of the door opening. An instant smile pulled her full mouth wide and lit her hazel eyes.

"Flint!" She rushed forward, full hips swaying, dark topknot bobbing, and threw her arms around him. She enveloped him not only in a big hug, but in a potent floral bouquet that was her trademark scent. "Terry said you'd be in this morning. It's been too long."

"I know...my fault. Good to see you, Linda."

She let go of him and turned to Nicky. "And you must be Flint's sister-in-law."

"Guilty. Nicky Keating." As the women shook hands, Nicky said, "And you were one of Flint's partners. I want to thank you for letting us use—"

"Hey, don't mention it." Linda waved a hand decorated with rings on each of her coral-tipped fingers. "Terry and I would do anything to help Flint. He just wouldn't let us before."

Linda's eyebrows arched as she gave him a questioning look that Flint ignored.

"So where's Terry?" he asked.

"He's out for a few hours on a case but said you should make yourself at home. That shouldn't be too hard—he's got your old office now, anyhow. Sher," she called to the blond receptionist, who was busy sorting through a file drawer. "*This* is Flint Armstrong. He's got the run of the place. Anything he needs, you get for him."

Her expression deadpan, the rail-thin Sher said, "Consider me your personal slave, Mr. Armstrong. Everyone else around here does." Obviously unimpressed, she went back to her sorting, muttering, "Coffee...morning paper...shoe shine..."

And Linda rolled her eyes. "Listen, I got an appointment in a few minutes, and I need to make a call first. If you're around at lunchtime, maybe we can break some bread together. Catch up, you know."

"Sounds good."

Like the whirlwind he remembered her to be, Linda was gone in a flash, disappearing into her office.

"She certainly has a lot of energy," Nicky said.

"Enough that she always kept Terry and me organized." He indicated the doorway on the other side of the reception area. "So let's get started."

His old office hadn't changed much. Same old-fashioned mahogany desk and chair. Same matching bookshelves. Same ancient filing cabinets he'd bought third-or fourth-hand. The computer equipment was up-to-date, however, and the personal effects were different. A corner of the desk held photographs of Terry's family. His wife's tawny complexion and tight cropped curls were duplicated in both of their kids.

Flint stared at the little girl who'd been born less than a year before Megan and hoped his old friend would never know what it was like to lose her. For a moment, he allowed himself to remember Megan's small arms wrapped around his neck....

Before he could get maudlin, Nicky broke into his thoughts. "So where do we begin?"

He took a deep breath and forced away the memory. "How computer literate are you?" he asked, feeling empty once more.

"I'm surviving the electronic information age... barely."

"Then we start with a couple of lessons on using search engines."

Sitting so close together before the computer made Flint a little uneasy. It reminded him of that moment the night before, when, in the process of securing him to the bed, Nicky had reached across him, their bodies coming into full contact.

His response had been instant. Powerful. Completely involuntary.

And very, *very* wrong.

Focusing on the work at hand, Flint showed Nicky how to access information about people from publications, then let her take over. Searching for Beverly Jensen resulted in thousands of references. When Nicky checked out the first dozen or so—the newest entries—articles about Beverly's death and the charges against Flint popped up.

"Not exactly what I had in mind," Nicky muttered.

"Unless you want to spend days going through each of these references, you have to narrow your search."

"Can we narrow it to Beverly and Eric?"

Flint showed her how, but doing so turned out to be a waste of time. Nothing linking Beverly and Eric in the same story.

"Whatever their history, it didn't make the news," Nicky said, voice rife with disappointment.

"I told you she never pressed charges until Eric violated the court order and roughed her up just recently. I'm sure she made a special effort to keep her personal life quiet, considering her job."

"But there are records," Nicky said.

"Which we can get to some other time by going down to Eleventh and State—the main office of the Chicago Police Department. So, what now?"

"I think we should check out Eric more thoroughly, but that can wait, too," Nicky said. "Since we're on Beverly, we might as well see what we can find about some of the more serious cases she prosecuted."

Because Nicky was a swift learner, Flint allowed her to take over completely. As far as he was concerned, she could search to her heart's content. She would feel useful and hopefully stop making demands on him.

Hearing someone behind him, he turned to find Terrence Clarke watching them from the doorway. With his thin frame encased in designer trousers, shirt and tie, his angular face bedecked with titanium eyeglasses, he might have passed for a yuppie if not for the long Rasta curls anchored at the nape of his neck.

Terry indicated he should step out of the room. Flint nodded.

"Nicky, Terry's here. I need to talk to him. Will you be all right on your own for a few minutes?"

"Uh-huh. Take your time."

Nicky was concentrating so hard that he figured she wouldn't even notice his absence. With a sense of relief, he left her to her own devices.

In the reception area, Terry clasped Flint's hand and slapped him in the shoulder. "My man! About time you came to your senses and stopped shutting Linda and me out."

Flint glanced back into the office where Nicky seemed to be glued to the computer screen. "I didn't have much choice in the matter."

Terry's "Ah, I see" left Flint with a weird feeling.

"Nothing to see, Clarke," he muttered, trying to convince himself that this was the truth. That his response to Nicky the night before was nothing more than an aberration.

"Let's talk in the conference room." As they crossed to the other side of the reception area, Terry called out, "Sher, two coffees, both black."

"Your wish is my command, master."

"Well, then, round up some corn bread...ham hocks...greens..."

"In your dreams."

Knowing that Terry was pulling Sher's chain—he wasn't the "soul food" type, Flint waited until they were out of her earshot before saying, "You found yourself a live one."

His ex-partner's mahogany face expressed his own amusement. "She got a mouth on her, but she's smart. I see bigger and better things for that lady 'round here, but don't quote me. I don't want her getting any more uppity." As they sat in upholstered chairs at the conference table, he sobered. ''You really got yourself backed into a corner, Armstrong. What's *your* version?''

Flint didn't spare himself. He placed the blame squarely on his own shoulders, from starting a relationship he wasn't yet ready for, to being responsible for Beverly's death. He also explained Phelps Rendell's defense strategy and the fact that Dr. Galloway would take the witness stand for him, providing she could prove to her own satisfaction that his sleep disorder was for real.

''That's something,'' Terry said. ''Better we clear your name.''

Delivering their coffees, Sher refrained from any wisecracks and whipped back out of the conference room with the speed of light. Flint suspected she'd overheard some of his story. Not that it mattered, since his life had become an open book to the press. All she had to do was read a newspaper or watch the nightly news.

''So how can I help?'' Terry asked.

''You already are helping.''

''What? Letting you use the computer and a few resources you couldn't find at the local library?''

''There's nothing more you can do.''

''What about contacts? And I can squeeze in some footwork time—''

''No need,'' Flint cut in. ''Truthfully, I don't really expect to incriminate anyone else.''

''But you're looking.''

''I agreed...to keep Nicky out of trouble.''

His gaze penetrating, Terry leaned back in his chair. ''So you're certain you killed this woman even though you don't remember squat?''

"*Killed* is a harsh way of putting it."

"Give me an option."

Flint only wished he had one. "All right, then—killed."

"Bull. I don't believe it."

"That's because you're my friend despite the fact that I've been a jerk this last year."

"A man carrying a load of grief," Terry amended. "Not the same thing. And because I am your friend as well as your ex-partner, I know your moral fibre better'n anyone. Sorry I don't buy into your being a murderer...not even one by misadventure."

"How else could Beverly have died?" Flint had asked himself that question over and over. "Rule out natural causes. Her neck was broken and she had a contusion at the base of her skull. The police think the corner of the dining room table was the likely weapon. I doubt she threw herself against it, then dragged herself back to bed before dying."

"Your sister-in-law has a theory 'bout someone else getting in your house."

"Nicky thinks a lot of things she shouldn't," Flint said, wondering about the things she *didn't* talk about. He would have to be blind, deaf and dumb not to have noticed how jumpy she got around him at times. He obviously scared her, but tough, loyal kid that she was, Nicky wasn't willing to admit it. "There weren't any signs of forced entry."

"Maybe you plumb forgot to lock the door."

"You know being careless isn't like me."

"These days, nothing much about you is like the old Flint. Your head ain't been on straight since the earthquake, my man. What makes you think you can't forget something simple, like locking a door?"

As much as Flint would have liked to believe Terry's point, he said, "That's highly unlikely, but I appreciate your good thoughts."

"Appreciate this—you don't prove otherwise and fast, you might not get a second chance at life. Remember, Illinois carries the death penalty."

Flint's stomach turned at the thought. "I haven't forgotten."

"And you're willing to stretch out your neck for the executioner without putting up a fight?"

Now why did that sentiment sound so familiar? "Is Nicky coaching you, or what?"

"Or what. I never thought I'd see the day when feeling sorry for yourself would be all you had going."

"Feeling sorry for *myself?*"

"What else would you call the way you been living? Or should I say *not* living?"

"I lost my family less than a year ago!"

"And that's a damn tragedy," Terry said. "But you survived. Get used to it and get on with...*something* worthwhile. Grief is natural. But ain't nothing natural about you losing your freedom or your own life to atone. And it won't bring Alana and Megan back. You're no murderer, Flint, not even if you were unconsciously responsible for what happened to the Jensen woman. But by not putting up the best fight you can to save yourself, you dishonor your wife and child's memories."

Flint recoiled as if Terry had just hit him. His ex-partner had never been this blunt before.

"You don't pull any punches."

"You never used to, either, my man," Terry said.

"I'll leave it be...for now. But you need me for anything, you remember I'm here."

"I'll keep that in mind."

With Terry's startling accusation echoing in his thoughts, Flint found it difficult to relax and socialize. He let Terry do some talking but was relieved when the other man had to depart to meet a client.

Returning to his former office, Flint found Nicky printing out a file. He watched her for a moment, studying her intense expression. She was a woman who fought for things. She was fighting for him. By doing any less, he wasn't only dishonoring Alana and Megan, but her as well.

Moving closer, he asked, "Find something interesting?"

She whipped around to face him, her expression triumphant. "You bet I did. Over the past few years, Beverly was successful in putting away half a dozen criminals with records of violent activities. I have a feeling about a gang-banger named Hector Villada. Take a look at this."

She handed him the printout.

Flint skimmed the story about Villada, who'd gone to jail for holding up a convenience store and pistol-whipping the clerk. He'd had a history of violence, including beating up on women. His live-in girlfriend had been sporting bruises when the police had made his arrest.

"No doubt Beverly had a particular interest in putting Villada behind bars. But what makes him stand out from the other scum she sent away?"

"Hector Villada was paroled for good behavior...just a week and a half before Christmas."

NICKY WAS SET on pursuing information on the gang-banger, and where better to get such than from the State's Attorney's Office? Having wanted to drop in anyway to learn more about Beverly's ex-husband, she saw this as a double-header opportunity. After lunch, once Linda Torres left them to their own devices, she suggested as much.

Flint shook his head. "Approaching anyone working for the prosecution is getting into a gray area."

His reluctance didn't really surprise her. "What could it hurt?" she asked, gathering her things from the extra chair at their table. "Certainly not your case."

"No one in that office will talk to me," he assured her. "I'm the bad guy, remember?"

"But *I'm* not," Nicky returned. She struggled with her jacket. One of the sleeves had turned inside out. "Maybe this is something I have to do alone."

Before she knew what he was about, Flint took charge of the jacket issue, releasing the sleeve. Nicky struggled into the garment, catching her breath when his fingers brushed the back of her neck.

What was wrong with her? Being unable to control her physical reactions to him was getting downright maddening!

Flint was asking, "Ever heard of being judged guilty by association?"

Gaze flickering across the cheek that was still slightly discolored from Jensen's punch, she stepped away from him to regain her mental balance.

"I'll take my chances. What can anyone do to me, anyway? Snub me? Big deal. No one's going to ride me out of town on a rail."

Getting him to agree to anything was like pulling teeth. But Nicky could be equally stubborn.

"I wasn't joking, Nicky. Get in the wrong face and you could be pegged as my accomplice."

The thought gave her a moment's pause. He was serious. She could read his concern in his expression and in the silver glitter of his eyes. Leading the way out of the restaurant into the crisp, cold air, she shook off the unease as quickly as he'd shoved it on her.

"Thinking I could be implicated is reaching, Flint. If I was guilty of anything, I wouldn't be poking my nose in their faces in the first place. You know at least a few of Beverly's co-workers. Isn't there someone you can name who might give you the benefit of the doubt and do some talking?"

Flint did come up with a name. "Marilyn Werner...Beverly's mentor."

"And that's a good thing?" she asked, incredulous. "I'd think someone close to Beverly would be especially eager to see you brought to justice."

"Probably. And she's a tough cookie to boot. But Beverly always said Marilyn was fair-minded, as well, that she examined a case from every angle even when the other A.S.A.'s were stuck on a single track."

"So what are we waiting for?"

Finding a pay phone on the street, Nicky made a call to ascertain that Marilyn Werner would be in the office that afternoon. They walked the few blocks to the State of Illinois Building. Flint agreed to wait for her in the lobby—an open-air, glass-paneled atrium that rose along the floors of government offices.

Nerves hit Nicky the moment she stepped into the elevator. Butterflies flitted around her stomach and she was having trouble taking a normal breath. But by the time she faced the gray-haired receptionist who held the keys to the kingdom, Nicky had calmed herself down.

Adopting her most charming smile, she said, "I'd like to see Marilyn Werner, please."

"You have an appointment?"

"No, but she'll want to see me. It's about the Beverly Jensen case."

"Beverly...?" The woman's mouth dropped open in surprise, and she took a moment to regain her composure. "Ms. Werner isn't handling that case."

"I know. But I won't speak to anyone else."

The receptionist rose. "I'll ask if she'll see you. Your name?"

"Nicole Keating."

Nicky waited on tenterhooks while the other woman slipped away from her desk and into a nearby office. The reception area being open to the atrium, Nicky wandered to the half-wall and looked down to where Flint sat on a bench, a lonely speck in a swarm of rushing people. She wondered if he gave her suspicions of Eric Jensen and Sid Shelton and Hector Villada any credence or if he was merely humoring her.

She also wondered what it would take to reintroduce him to his old self.

Wishing she could give him back his life in its entirety, Nicky didn't realize the receptionist had returned until the woman came directly to her.

"Ms. Werner will see you now."

A minute later, she was seated across from the tough cookie herself. Beverly's mentor was dressed in a charcoal-gray suit sans any accessory that would soften its severity. Her short black hair was styled away from her face, revealing a single thick strand of silver. She looked to be all business.

Removing a pair of half-moon reading glasses, the prosecutor said, "I understand you have information for me about the Jensen case."

Nicky's stomach knotted. Time to face the music. "Actually, what I said was that it was *about* the Jensen case. I was hoping to get information from you."

"You what? Ms. Keating, I'm a busy civil servant with more cases than I care to—"

"I'm not here to waste your time," Nicky cut in. "I'm as interested in justice as you are."

"Justice for whom?"

"Flint Armstrong."

The prosecutor's gaze narrowed. "Who are you?"

"His sister-in-law."

Recognition flared in her cool blue eyes. "I thought you looked familiar. I have nothing to say to you, Ms. Keating. You'll have to leave."

When Nicky didn't rush right out, the prosecutor reached for the telephone. Fearing the woman was about to call security, Nicky lunged forward and covered her hand.

"No—please, hear me out. Beverly said you were fair-minded, that you investigated angles that other A.S.A.'s might skip."

"The Jensen case isn't mine."

"But Beverly was your friend." When she felt the hand under hers go slack, Nicky let go and sank into her seat. "Unless I'm mistaken, you have a special interest in seeing that the right person is brought to justice."

"What makes you think Flint Armstrong isn't that person?"

"Knowing him. I've never met anyone with better ethics or a stronger sense of responsibility." Strong enough to blame himself for an act of God. "Think about it. He called the police to report Beverly's death. If he'd deliberately killed her, why would he have made that call? Why would he have killed her in his own home?"

"Crimes of passion never make sense."

"But he could have moved her body afterward," Nicky continued. "Pretended he knew nothing."

"Knowing nothing *is* his story."

"No. His not being able to *remember* isn't the same thing." Not that she was going to say a word about the sleeping disorder. "But in their enthusiasm to avenge Beverly Jensen, both the police and your own office acted irresponsibly, accusing and charging Flint Armstrong with murder without so much as considering any other possible suspects."

"Like whom?"

"Any criminal who had reason to hate a successful prosecutor...like Hector Villada."

"Who is safely behind bars."

Her words took Nicky aback. "Hector Villada was paroled for good behavior two weeks ago—plenty of time to plan and execute a murder. How could you not know?"

Marilyn Werner didn't try to cover her surprise. "A couple of weeks ago...I was out of town for a while. And I've been so busy...somehow I missed the news." A horrified expression crossed her face. "Villada said he would even the score when he got out."

Feeling vindicated, Nicky took a deep breath and asked, "What if Villada wasn't making idle talk?

Can't you give Flint the benefit of the doubt long enough to find out?''

"I told you this isn't my case. Dean Lowry is handling it.''

"Then speak to him.''

The prosecutor closed her eyes and shook her head. "Believe me, the only thing that interests Lowry is chalking up another conviction with as little muss and fuss as possible.''

"But *you're* interested in getting it right, aren't you?'' Nicky asked. "You can find out if Villada disclosed any plans about Beverly to the other inmates while he was in prison...or to his homies since. What about prodding the police to investigate his movements?''

"Without cause? Without Lowry's cooperation? Not hardly.''

"Then *I'll* get someone to investigate.'' Nicky was ready to go after the creep herself. "You have access to information on Villada—his address, his associates. Give me anything you have and I'll run with it.''

The A.S.A.'s fingers were already flying over her computer keyboard. "I can't give you any personal data. It would be a violation of Villada's civil rights.''

Nicky watched the computer screen as the picture and profile of a young Hispanic man with long black hair came up. A moment later, the printer spit out hard copy—an enlargement of the mug shot. The prosecutor handed it to Nicky.

"This you can have,'' she said, rising. "As for the personal information, you do understand that I can't give that to you.'' She headed for the door. "Excuse me, but I have to check for messages at the front desk. I'll only be gone for a moment.''

A moment was long enough for Nicky to get a good look at the monitor and Villada's background profile. Hurriedly, she scribbled down his former Logan Square address and made a few other notes on the back of the copied photograph.

Which was exactly what Marilyn Werner had intended, Nicky was certain. Why else would the prosecutor leave her alone with the information on the screen?

"Sorry to keep you waiting, Ms. Keating."

Forewarned by the voice from the hall, Nicky sat back, folded the photo and slipped it into her pocket even as Marilyn Werner returned empty-handed.

"Is there anything else I can do for you?" she asked, taking the chair behind her desk.

"Eric Jensen—how much do you know about him?"

"That he's a monster parading in the guise of a human being—barely a step up from Villada, though as far as I know, the way he earns his living is legal."

"I don't like him, either."

"You've met, then?"

"We haven't exactly been introduced, but I've seen him in action."

The prosecutor nodded. "Ah, the wake."

"Exactly."

"I left before you and Mr. Armstrong arrived, but I heard about the episode later."

"Including the part where Jensen made some not-so-veiled threats against Flint?"

The other woman nodded. "He was good at making threats...and at carrying them out." She shook her head. "I'll never understand why women stay with their abusers so long. I can't tell you how few bring charges against the men.''

''Beverly among them.''

''Unfortunately. Some misguided sense of loyalty, I suppose. At least she finally came to her senses and divorced the bastard.''

''Which didn't stop him from stalking her,'' Nicky said. ''Or roughing her up.'' Getting to her point, she took a deep breath and plunged into it. ''I was wondering—and maybe you were, too—about how far a man supposedly still in love with his ex-wife would go to stop her from being with anyone else.''

''Based on nearly twenty years' experience in this office?'' Marilyn Werner appeared appropriately pensive when she said, ''Murder, Ms. Keating. Murder.''

Chapter Seven

Flint was pacing, imagining the worst that could be happening to Nicky in the State's Attorney's Office, when he finally caught sight of her stepping off an elevator. Chest constricted with apprehension, he met her halfway. Though he wanted to take her in his arms and just hold her for a moment, he shoved his hands into his jacket pockets instead.

"At least they didn't detain you as an accessory."

"Nope. They sure didn't."

A smile played around the corners of her mouth, then blossomed into a wide grin. Gathering she hadn't gotten herself into hot water, after all, Flint felt the tightness rush out of him like a balloon whose air had just been released.

"What?" he asked.

She flourished a blowup of a mug shot. "Voilà! Meet Hector Villada."

Unconvinced that the ex-con had anything to do with Beverly's death, Flint took the photograph from her and examined it dispassionately. Villada was a pretty boy with long hair, a pouty mouth and soulful eyes—undoubtedly what attracted the women he'd then abused.

"Turn it over," Nicky urged. "I got Villada's last known address and some information on his mother and one of his old cronies."

Flint gave the notations a cursory look as she explained how she'd obtained the personal information.

"I'm sure Phelps will be impressed."

Voice ripe with annoyance, she asked, "Meaning you're not?" and snatched the paper out of his hand.

Choosing to keep his doubts to himself, he hedged a bit. "You always impress me, Nicky." That was the truth.

And it seemed to settle her down.

"I was thinking we should talk to Mr. Rendell in person," Nicky said. "Bring him up to speed."

"Fine by me."

"Maybe his investigator dug up something on Eric Jensen or Sid Shelton."

Knowing from experience Phelps hadn't had enough time to get anything definitive, Flint figured the wisest course was to keep his own counsel. He wasn't going to be the one to burst Nicky's bubble.

A light snow lazily drifted down on them as they set out for the lawyer's office, about a five-minute walk from the State of Illinois Building. Nicky lifted her face to the sky and took a big breath, expressing her obvious enjoyment.

Flint enjoyed watching *her*. The cold had put color in her cheeks and snowflakes stuck to her thick eyelashes. When her gaze met his, her eyes sparkled and her mouth trembled into a dazzling smile that lit their bit of the universe. An odd feeling enveloped him and he wondered that he'd never before realized how beautiful she was.

Not the sleek beauty of an Alana, perhaps...but a sunny, appealing comeliness that was uniquely Nicky.

When they crossed the street, Flint placed a protective hand in the middle of her back. Nicky ducked her head and walked a bit faster, then started to chatter as if trying to cover a sudden attack of nerves.

"Marilyn Werner's on our side. If we come up with something impressive, she'll probably make Dean Lowry sit up and take notice."

"She thinks I'm innocent?"

Nicky made a dismissive gesture. "Not exactly, but once I got through to her, she was willing to give you the benefit of the doubt."

"Are you sure you didn't bully the poor woman into saying whatever it was you wanted to hear?"

Nicky narrowed her gaze at him. "I doubt that anyone can bully Marilyn Werner into anything. I merely gave her some logical options. As you said, she's interested in all the angles. Too bad this case wasn't assigned to her in the first place. She wouldn't have been so quick to bring charges against you."

"Maybe," a doubtful Flint said. Even he had to admit the charges had been logical considering the circumstances. "So what did she say about Hector Villada?"

"That he threatened Beverly. He meant to even the score when he got out."

"I imagine it's not unusual for a convicted criminal to make an empty threat."

"If it *was* empty."

He could tell Nicky's batteries were charged about Villada, so he didn't press the point. "Did you get anything from Marilyn about Beverly's ex?"

"Her profound hatred of the man. Plus his home

and business addresses. She asked that we keep her informed of anything we learn.''

''I'll just bet she did.''

That way, the prosecution could have the same information as the defense, Flint knew, and be prepared with a counterattack. Any data that Phelps intended to use would have to be disclosed anyway, but mainlining it to the State's Attorney's Office would give them a head start. He feared Nicky had a lot to learn about how real life worked.

Phelps Rendell's law firm was located in a new high-rise office complex that curved with the bend of the Chicago River where it split into branches. They were shown directly into his office, decorated in tones of gray, including the leather seating arrangement and lacquered furniture. The only bolder color came from his prized possessions—Flint knew the century-old, hand-tied rug from the Orient had belonged to a sultan, and the painting whose focus was a brilliant red poppy was an original Georgia O'Keeffe.

Once seated, Phelps asked, ''So, Flint, how are the nerves?''

''About…?''

''Your coming night being wired and watched over.''

Having shoved his appointment at the sleep disorder center to the back of his mind, Flint had nearly forgotten it. ''Whatever happens, happens.''

Phelps frowned at Nicky. ''I thought you were going to work on him.''

She sighed. ''Flint's a tough nut, but he is cracking. He's been amazingly cooperative today.''

As if just realizing how much, she gazed at him with

suspicion. Flint countered with an expression of innocence.

"All kidding aside," Phelps said, "I got my answer about Sid Shelton's appearance at court this morning."

"Another chop shop incident?" Flint asked.

"Nothing on him. Nor was he a witness in any other prosecution. As far as I can tell, he had absolutely no official reason to be there."

"His reason was Flint," Nicky said, sounding satisfied with herself.

Even though Shelton's appearance could have been coincidence, Flint accepted the likelihood that she was correct in this instance. But to what purpose? Had Shelton merely chosen to hassle an old nemesis after all this time—it had been nearly a year and a half since ACT had gotten the goods on him—or could the car parts dealer have a more recent and compelling motivation?

Nicky's theory about Sid Shelton targeting him for murder but killing Beverly because she caught him inside the house seemed too far-fetched to be believable.

"What about Eric Jensen?" she was asking. "Did your investigators get anything on him?"

"Other than what you already know?" Phelps shook his head. "They'll keep working on it, but don't expect miracles."

"I have addresses and phone numbers for him."

As Phelps took notes, she told him how she'd obtained the information at the State's Attorney's Office. Then she handed him the mug shot.

"You can add Hector Villada to your list of suspects," she said. "I found an article about his being paroled for good behavior after Beverly put him away for armed robbery and pistol-whipping the store clerk. He's been out for two weeks...and Marilyn Werner admitted he'd vowed to get even with Beverly when he was released.'' She pointed to the print that, after a cursory inspection, the lawyer had dropped on his desk. ''I'd like to keep that, so maybe you can have someone make a copy.''

Phelps seemed indifferent. ''It won't hurt to keep one on file in case we need it later,'' he said. ''The more alternative suspects we can drum up to take the heat off Flint—put doubt in the minds of the jury members—the better. But I'll be honest here. I'm not convinced we should waste our time tracking down Hector Villada.''

Nicky sounded amazed when she said, ''I don't understand.''

''First, it's not unusual that, in the heat of the moment, a convicted felon will threaten the police or prosecutors responsible for incarcerating him. But it rarely happens, because when he's released, he's cooled down and he wants to stay far away from representatives of the system that can send him back to prison, maybe permanently this time.''

Flint recognized the frustration in Nicky's posture and expression. He'd tried to warn her....

''But if we can find someone who heard him threaten Beverly,'' she argued, ''either in prison or on the streets—''

''I'm telling you it's a waste of energy,'' Phelps cut in. ''Gang-bangers don't hide in shadows and make neat kills. If Hector Villada were responsible for Beverly Jensen's death, he wouldn't have acted alone. He would have made a show of breaking into her home to get at her...if he didn't cut her down on the streets in a drive-by execution. Believe me, her death wouldn't have been pretty."

Flint flinched. "Death is never pretty." As he well knew firsthand.

He glanced at Nicky, who sank back into her chair and clamped her jaw tight. No doubt about her being decidedly unhappy with the lawyer's decision.

Figuring he'd get the brunt of her displeasure on the way home, Flint prepared himself for a bumpy ride.

THE ELEVATED TRAIN slowed for a torturous curve that jostled them into other passengers who were trying to remain upright by hanging onto seat backs and metal poles. The late-afternoon rush hour had begun, and they hadn't been able to get seats. It was too crowded and too hot. The metallic screech of wheels against tracks scraped up Nicky's spine. Tension escalating, she couldn't hold in her resentment any longer.

Aiming her words up at Flint, she said, "I thought lawyers were supposed to follow a client's wishes."

"When it's in their best interests," Flint agreed. "Besides, technically speaking, you're not Phelps Rendell's client."

No. She'd merely contacted Phelps to take his case and then had bullied Flint into hiring the legal eagle.

"I thought we were supposed to be in this to-gether," she complained.

"I'm not playing a game of one-upmanship with you, if that's what you think."

"But you didn't back me, either. And after you said Phelps would be impressed."

"I think he was, on one level, but he's being real-istic. He did make some valid points about Villada."

With which Flint obviously agreed.

"Well," Nicky said, "if Rendell won't follow up on Hector Villada..."

"What?" he asked over more screeching of metal against metal.

She waited until they'd rounded the curve, then watching closely for his reaction, said, "*We* can follow up."

Caution shadowed his eyes when he asked, "How?"

"By putting the information I got from Marilyn Werner to good use."

"You mean try to find him on his own turf?" His voice rose in a fusion of amazement and ire. "A gangbanger? Are you out of your mind?"

Nicky stiffened. Another criticism about her judgment. She hadn't forgotten Flint's greeting after all she'd gone through to bail him out.

Aware that several bystanders were now staring and straining to hear their conversation, she said, "I must be crazy to help someone who won't even help himself."

"Nicky, give this up," Flint pleaded. "Villada's no one to fool around with."

"Exactly my point." So why did both men want to dismiss him out of hand? "Working in a public high school, I've dealt with gang-bangers every day for more than five years. I'm not afraid. If we can find out—"

"No!" He cut her dead. "You *should* be afraid. I'm not going along with this."

"Fine."

The train screeched to a stop and the doors opened. One woman who'd been listening seemed reluctant to exit, but as Nicky glared at her, she stepped out the doors and rushed to the other side of the platform where another train was waiting. At least their car had emptied some and though they still didn't have seats, they were no longer cheek-by-jowl with strangers.

Nicky waited until their train was moving again before saying, "You don't want to go with me? Then don't. I'll go alone."

Flint's forehead furrowed, the scar from the earthquake standing out in stark relief. She hated the fact that, while he made her angry and resentful, he had the ability to draw her in, to make her long for something that wasn't to be.

"Don't be foolish, Nicky. Give it some time. You'll see Phelps and I are correct. You're just angry because you feel like you've wasted a day's research."

That he was again criticizing her didn't get past Nicky. To hear him talk, nothing she ever did was right...it reminded her of her mother's lifelong attitude.

Unable to help herself, she said, "Better than wasting my life."

He glowered but didn't make any denials.

Nicky couldn't care less about a day wasted. She was angry because neither man was taking her seriously. Really, because Flint wasn't. Here she'd thought he was finally involved in what was happening to him and appreciated her concern. She'd been thinking of them as a team, while he'd undoubtedly been doing nothing more than humoring her all day—a suspicion she'd been harboring since she'd realized he'd been a little too cooperative to be believed.

Unwilling to continue the argument any longer, however, she kept her own counsel.

The silence between them stretched thin as the train descended from the elevated tracks to surface level right before their stop. But Nicky could be as stubborn as anyone. Even him. That he didn't try to pick up some safe conversation on the short walk to her place both annoyed and disappointed her.

Just before entering the vestibule, Nicky happened to glance over her shoulder. She started. Parked a few buildings down was the same silver Buick she'd spotted the day before. Again, a shadowy figure sat unmoving in the driver's seat. A man, she was certain.

But was he a neighbor? A visitor?

Or a reporter as she'd first suspected?

In a fine mood, she waved, silently challenging whoever it was to get out of his car and approach them. While outwardly controlled, inside she was spoiling for a fight. She would have liked nothing better than to tell off some jerky tabloid newshound who wouldn't think twice about running a story that would hurt people.

But if the Buick's driver caught her signal, he ignored it.

"A friend of yours?" Flint asked.

"Not hardly."

Without explaining, she swept by him into the vestibule, unlocked the downstairs door and rushed up the stairs. By the time she unlocked her apartment door, she had a new plan—one that involved the animal that now attacked her with such simple enthusiasm.

Ruffling his silly-looking ears, she said, "Scraps, *outside!*"

The dog lunged away from her and after his leash.

"I can walk him," Flint volunteered.

"No need. I could use the exercise," she countered coolly.

Scraps dropped the leash at their feet and looked from one human to another as if waiting for them to decide who would have the honor.

"Then I'll come with you."

Flint's tagging along would throw a wrench into things, Nicky thought with frustration, as she clipped the leash to the dog's collar. He *was* bigger and stronger than she was. He could physically stop her from going anywhere. Now what?

When the phone rang at that exact second, she blessed her luck. "You'd better get it. It could be Rendell or the sleep disorder center."

"More likely it's for you."

Whipping out to the landing with the dog, she said, "Then take a message."

Flint grumbled but didn't decline.

Focused on her objective, Nicky rushed out of the building and toward her car, jerking to a stop only when Scraps found a tree particularly interesting. Nerves on edge, she checked her apartment windows, knowing Flint could look down at them at any moment. No familiar face. So far, so good.

To encourage the dog to hurry, she said, "Car ride!"

Scraps barked in agreement.

A moment later she was in the driver's seat, the dog happily ensconced in back, his excitement whistling through his nose. With some trepidation, she started off, so distracted as she passed the silver Buick that she didn't think to take a gander at the driver until it was too late. No matter her protests about being able to take care of herself, she wished Flint had agreed to accompany her.

The sun had set and dusk was rapidly descending as she sped to Logan Square. She parked a few buildings down from the address that had been Hector Villada's before he'd been incarcerated. Exiting the car, she brought Scraps with her...not that a forty-pound dog could offer much protection if she got herself into trouble. But his companionship gave her more confidence.

Though she was less than three miles from home, Nicky knew she'd entered a world with different rules.

One being *view strangers with suspicion,* which was brought home to her clearly when she tried talking to a pregnant woman with two small children in tow.

"Excuse me, but do you know Hector Villada?" she asked, restraining the dog from sniffing the kids, who clung to their mother's side.

The woman's dark eyes flickered—with recognition at the name, Nicky suspected—but she shook her head, muttered something in Spanish and fled to the entrance of the building next to the one Nicky sought.

Not that she even knew how she'd react if she actually *found* the gang-banger—coming face-to-face with Villada was the last thing she wanted. Rather, she'd been hoping to get some information on what he'd been up to since being released from prison. Maybe find out if he'd made any threats against Beverly Jensen.

The neighborhood was edgy, gang signs decorating some of the larger apartment buildings. Villada's former residence was in disrepair. Windows stared out onto the courtyard with vacant eyes. Others, ringed by the black soot of a recent fire, had been boarded up.

She entered the properly numbered vestibule anyway.

A glance at the mailboxes disclosed no Villadas. And though she tried each of the six buzzers, no one answered.

Wandering back out into the courtyard, Nicky wondered if she should check for tenants at one of the other entrances. A creepy feeling—as if someone were watching her—settled the question. Even as she raced for the car, she took a good look around. No one that she could see—the area being dark but for the pools of illumination from the streetlights. Even figuring her imagination was undoubtedly playing with her, she wasn't hanging around any longer than necessary.

"C'mon, Scraps."

But the dog had gotten too interested in the new territory to instantly cooperate. The sound of feet slapping against pavement made her flip around, but it was only a middle-aged man, probably returning from work. Still, the dog's delaying her departure when she wanted to be gone made Nicky realize she should have left him in the Escort.

That was exactly what she did at her next stop, only three blocks away. Parking her car, Nicky wondered if she was being foolhardy for persisting. Normally, she wouldn't have chosen to test her mettle after dark in a neighborhood where looking over her shoulder came naturally. She could have kicked Flint for riling her into doing something so imprudent.

Besides, the prospect of facing Villada's mother alone was unsettling. With trepidation, she approached the well-lit house, that was asphalt-sided, curls of peeling paint hanging from the trim. She stood before the slanted steps for a moment, wondering how she could question a mother about her son's criminal activities.

With great finesse, Nicky decided, racing up to the porch before she could change her mind. She pressed the buzzer.

The low sound of an engine cruising behind her whipped Nicky around in time to see a car speed up. Streetlights shone off a pale finish, but before she could get a better look, the front door of the house opened.

"Who're you?" a little boy demanded.

"Juanito, you know Mama says don't open the door to no strangers." She pushed her brother off. "Now go watch television."

Dark eyes in a young face promising great beauty gazed with suspicion at Nicky...

Who promptly asked, "Is your mother in?"

"You from social services?"

"No, but I'd like to talk to her."

Hugging the half-closed door, the teenage girl waited, full mouth pursed.

"About Hector," Nicky added as if they were old acquaintances.

"What's my brother done now?"

Nicky feigned ignorance. "Nothing bad, I hope."

"He's not here."

"What about your mother?"

"Working. Second job. You wanna know something about Hector, you ask me."

"Do you know where he is?"

She shook her head. "Ain't seen him for a while. Maybe Isabelle knows."

Isabelle was the name of the live-in girlfriend, according to the article, Nicky remembered. The one he'd sent to the hospital. Obviously that hadn't proved to be a deterrent to their relationship.

"Isabelle Rodriguez? Where can I find her?"

"A block over," the girl said, pointing northwest, "on Milwaukee. She works in a place called Tito's next to the Polish deli."

In the background, a baby started crying. Another sibling or the teenager's own child? Nicky wondered.

"Gotta go."

The girl closed the door before Nicky could manage a simple "Thank you."

In this part of town, Milwaukee Avenue was a busy commercial strip. Since it was doubtful that she'd find parking any closer, Nicky started walking. Her city smarts kept her alert, but while the uneasy sensation of being watched followed her, the only people she spotted seemed to be workers returning home. The sky was flaking again, enough to make the footing a tad slippery.

Finding the Polish deli, she rounded its corner entrance and slowed to catch her breath, at which point she confronted the nature of Isabelle's work.

Emblazoned in neon fuchsia and lime-green lettering, TITO'S TATTOOS flashed at her.

Nicky took a peak through the window. Inside, a slight, ponytailed tattoo artist was finishing a job. The burly customer's back—a network of colored lines and designs—quickly disappeared beneath a thick sweater. Unable to help wondering how much of the man's anatomy was illustrated, she entered as he pulled on a jacket and sauntered toward the door.

"See you next month, Tito."

Avoiding looking at the needles he was throwing away, Nicky concentrated on the owner himself. His features were striking, almost as if he were wearing makeup.

"Excuse me, but I'm looking for Isabelle Rodriguez."

Tito's thick-lashed gaze swept over her. "Get in line, sweetcakes."

"She works here, right?"

"Not no more she don't," he said with a touch of indignation. "She ain't been in the past week. I guess you could say she resigned."

Not in for a week…since Beverly Jensen's death?

Grabbing on to the connection, she asked, "You wouldn't know where I could find her?"

"You need information? I need new customers." His long, manicured fingers stroked a fresh packet of needles. "Take a seat, sweetcakes."

Nicky wasn't about to despoil her virgin skin in trade for an address. "U-uh, no thanks. I prefer keeping my artwork to my walls."

"Then how about I do your eyes—liner and shadow—and your lips, too? You can get up every morning looking naturally beautiful."

Or like a hooker.

Nicky suddenly realized *his* features were enhanced by tattooing rather than makeup. "I kind of like the way I look now. About Isabelle—"

"My way of thinking, everyone could use some extra help."

Because he was staring at her as if she were a guinea pig—and she was certain she wouldn't get anything out of him unless she let him experiment on her—Nicky edged out of the store so fast she didn't have time to look where she was going. Smacking into another body stopped her cold.

"Hey, watch it, lady!"

Nicky started. "Sorry." The teenage girl's face was painted to look so artificial that she might have indulged in Tito's deluxe makeover.

A guy wearing a cap, bill turned to the left, and a leather starter jacket, open despite the cold and falling snow, draped a casual arm across the girl's shoulders. "You all right, Madonna?"

"I dunno, Julio. This bitch stepped on my foot."

"But not on purpose," Nicky swore, growing uneasy enough to back away from the two until a third youth behind her made her freeze.

"Your kind thinks you can come into our neighborhood and do whatever you want."

He, too, was wearing a starter jacket and a tilted billed cap. Nicky recognized them as gang-bangers. Her mouth went dry. Were they merely out for her wallet...or a cheap thrill? Or could they be friends of Hector Villada, set on her by his younger sister?

Heart in her throat, she played for time. "I meant no disrespect." And prayed for a source of help.

"You believe that?" the kid behind her asked.

Madonna looked thoughtful, then shook her head. "Bitch is lying."

While the street was loaded with vehicles, the drivers were focused on traffic. And people on foot were scarce, hurrying, paying them no mind. Nicky wondered how much Tito's full treatment cost—and whether or not it included escort service to her vehicle. But when she glanced into the storefront, the interior was dark and the owner had vanished. She started to sweat beneath her layers of clothing.

The one named Julio said, "Maybe we oughta teach her a lesson."

Thinking fast, Nicky picked up on the implication. "I *am* a teacher." Quickly identifying the local high school, she stared at Julio and bluffed. "At Clemente." Just maybe she could make him think twice about messing with someone who might be able to I.D. him. "Julio...? Didn't I have you in one of my classes last year?"

The other boy snorted. "*Him* go to school?"

"Shut up, Nestor."

"You two, stop screwin' around and grab her!" Madonna ordered.

Nicky yelled loud as she made her move, but the sound was swallowed by the raucous bass blare of rap music pouring out of the open window of a passing van. Nestor grabbed her upper arm to stop her and shoved a hand over her mouth. She bit into his flesh, but spilling curses into her ear, he hung on until he'd pulled her around the corner onto the poorly lit side street, the alley mere steps away.

Nicky put some of those defense moves Flint had laughed at to good use. Stomping on an instep here, jabbing an elbow there, she freed herself. But before she could make a run for it, Madonna stepped in her way.

Nicky lunged to the right, but Julio cut her off. To the left, Nestor waited. And behind her, the deserted alley loomed like a tomb.

They began to close in on her.

Madonna withdrew something from her pocket that glittered under the flat blue light. "Let's see how you like the tattoo I'm gonna give you with this." She brandished a thin blade before Nicky's eyes.

"Let me do it," Julio said.

"No, me!" Nestor insisted.

Ordering herself not to panic, Nicky snap-kicked Madonna in the knee and lunged past the crumpling girl, right elbow aimed as a weapon. But from behind, cruel fingers closed around her throat and spun her around so fast on the snow-slippery pavement that Nicky couldn't keep to her feet.

Even as Julio threw her down to the pavement, Nestor flew past her—literally, feet off the ground—and, with a gurgling sound, came face-to-face with a brick wall. Madonna screeched epithets and Nicky focused on the man who planted himself protectively at her side.

Face twisted in a feral snarl, Flint demanded, "Now which one of you wimps is going to make my day?"

Chapter Eight

"Wimps!" echoed the gang-banger who'd nearly strangled Nicky. "You know who you're talkin' to?"

Flint looked each of them square in the eye and laced his low return with menace. "The real question is—do you know who *I* am?"

Aware of Nicky staggering to her feet beside him, he had to trust that she wasn't hurt to keep himself from reaching out to help her. Should he let his guard slip for even a second, they would be all over him.

Besides which, if he so much as touched her, he wasn't sure he could keep his head where it needed to be...on *them*.

A knife suddenly appeared in the leader's fist. "Watcha gonna do now, *big man?*" the creep asked, casually tossing the weapon from one hand to the other.

"Before you point that blade at me, you'd better know what *I* have here," Flint warned, slipping his hand into his jacket pocket.

"Julio!" the girl yelled, eyes fastening on the bulge. "He got a gun."

"He's bluffing, Madonna."

"You don't know that."

"Three to one—we can take him," the injured one boasted, while blood from his nose trickled down to his chin. He covertly moved his hand behind him.

"Touch it," Flint warned him, "and I'm through playing games."

The thug froze with his hand halfway back. No doubt he *was* carrying and had stuck the weapon in his waistband under the starter jacket.

"Hey, this ain't no matter of honor," Madonna told her companions. "Julio, let it go...okay?"

Seeming torn, Julio finally said, "Yeah, why not? We ain't being paid enough for none of us to get hurt anyhow."

"Paid?" Nicky repeated.

He backed off into the alley, the other two following his lead.

"Who paid you? Hector?"

But the gang members were already slipping into the shadows.

"Was it Hector Villada?" she yelled.

"Nicky, let it go."

Flint merely put a hand on her shoulder to bring her to her senses in case she had any ideas to go after them. The next thing he knew, she was flying *at him*, throwing herself against his chest, wrapping her arms around his neck.

Her "Omigod!" was muffled against his jacket.

Nicky was trembling against him, and Flint did the only thing possible. He wrapped his arms around her back and held her close. Her shudder shot through him, igniting a response that was purely physical. His heart pounded—partially from his anxiety for her safety, but mostly from an attraction that he'd somehow managed to deny for too long. And when she raised her frightened face to his, a single tear rolling down her cheek, he did the only thing possible.

He kissed her.

Not a peck on her forehead or a brush across her lips, but a real man-to-woman connection.

Her mouth was soft...sweet...salty from the single tear that mingled between their lips.

Flint explored deeper until he could no longer tell where he ended and Nicky began. Her hands stole up into the hair lying over his collar, her fingers twining with the strands, tugging as if she could pull from him what she needed. A small sound contained deep in her throat nearly undid him.

She stole his breath away...put wings to his soul...mainlined a fever into his very blood. And when she pulled away with a gasp, he wanted to force her back to him...stamp her with his mark...make her his.

But the way Nicky was staring at him...wide-eyed and openmouthed...

He loosened his grasp and took a step back, the small movement throwing up an invisible wall between them. He could see her, but as if a sheet of glass separated them, he could no longer touch her.

Clenching his jaw hard, he stepped back again.

"Sorry," he muttered, his features so stiff they might have been frozen despite the mild winter night. "I guess I got carried away."

"Right." Nicky averted her gaze as if she couldn't bear to look directly at him. "Carried away...by the unusual circumstances..."

So they were agreed.

So why the hell did that make him feel lousy?

"Let's get out of here," Flint growled. "I'll drive you to your car."

And he would make certain that he didn't repeat *this* mistake.

STUNNED AND CONFUSED, Nicky stiffly sat in the passenger seat of Flint's old Pontiac waiting for him to say something—anything—that would make her feel better. She wouldn't even care if he lectured her about being right. But a weird silence stretched between them as he started up the engine.

What had just happened?

One minute, Flint had been kissing her like there was no tomorrow...the next he'd seemed embarrassed and angry with himself for touching her. He'd *apologized,* for heaven's sake, as if he'd done something wrong! Nicky gulped and considered the unacceptable.

What if he'd somehow transferred his feelings for Alana onto her before realizing who he was holding in his arms?

The notion got to her...made her stomach churn...left her feeling empty inside.

And belligerent.

Nicky suddenly resented Flint's last-minute change of heart that sent him chasing after her. So what if he'd gotten her out of a serious predicament? She told herself that she could have handled the situation herself. After all, she'd broken up more than one gang fight at school. She'd been thrown for a moment, but she would have recouped.

Half-convinced of that, she snapped, "How did you know where to find me anyway?" as Flint pulled away from the curb.

"I have a good memory," he said calmly, as if he'd

missed her sharp tone. "The addresses on the back of Villada's mug shot. I cruised his old place, but when I didn't see your car, I figured you must have gone on to see his mother."

"She was working."

"I never got that far in my conversation with his sister. My showing up right after you did must have freaked the kid out. She slammed the door in my face. I knew you were around, though, because I spotted the Escort. By the way, Scraps isn't too happy at being dragged into this situation just to be left alone in a cold car. What if something had happened to you and you weren't able to get back to him? He could have frozen to death."

Nicky ignored the immediate twinge of guilt over the dog. "It's not that cold and unlike me, he wears a fur coat." She was charged up, determined to get her shot in. "So you rode around after me in your trusty white charger, arriving in the nick of time to save the day...which you would never have had to do if you'd agreed to cooperate in the first place."

From the silence that followed, it seemed that she'd succeeded.

Then he asked, "Is that gratitude I hear?"

"About as much as you've given me."

She could have sworn Flint ground his teeth together, and he was practically snarling at her when he said, "No more heroics, Nicky."

"Why?" She couldn't help mocking him. "Are you all out?"

"I meant *you*. I want you to stay out of trouble."

"Does that also mean you'll come with me next time?"

He cursed.

"Does it?" she persisted as they pulled up next to her parked car.

Inside, Scraps was alert to their presence and seemed to be fine if impatient.

"I'll agree to consider your point of view," Flint said, voice tight, "if you agree not to be reckless and go off half-cocked on your own."

Registering the *half-cocked* complaint, she repeated, *"Consider?"*

"All right. Seriously consider."

Feeling as if she'd won a victory of sorts, Nicky said, "Deal," and opened the passenger door.

"You're going straight home, right?"

Glaring at him, she merely traded his car for hers, calming the enthusiastic animal who tried to climb in her lap. The only thing about Scraps that seemed cold was his nose, a pretty normal dog condition as far as she was concerned. Flint was waiting for her—impatiently, no doubt—and once she hit the road, he stuck close behind her.

The last of her annoyance with him fading, Nicky realized how positive the past hour had been despite her frightening experience.

Flint had chosen to come after her—an active decision on his part—after which he'd faced down the teenage thugs like a man possessed. Whatever his reason, he'd followed the instinct to kiss her. And then for once they'd argued about something other than his lack of motivation.

To her satisfaction, he was acting like anything but his recent, uninvolved self. Rather, he was more like the old Flint she recalled. And a bit of a Flint she hadn't known existed, Nicky admitted.

She was still amazed—thrilled, even—by Flint's

fierce countenance and stance when he'd challenged the gang for her. She felt as if she'd been watching a movie or something, for surely this hadn't been real life.

Not *her* life.

But it had happened for real.

Flint was coming out of himself. Fighting back. He was even looking better, more alive and without the pallor that had made him seem so drained the day she'd dragged him home against his will. And that had been only two days before, she marveled, happily perceiving there was hope for him yet.

By the time they found parking spots down the block from her building, Nicky realized she was in an exceptionally good humor considering all that she'd been through that day. And, as he joined her, Flint seemed calm, his truculent expression having disappeared. She didn't miss the fact that he took a thorough look around, however, as if he were keeping an eye out for more trouble.

Ignoring the shiver that leaped up her spine, she said, "Since you have your car now, I guess you won't need a ride to the sleep disorder center."

Not that he needed her to take him in the first place. Public transportation would drop him off at the Lakeshore Medical Center's front door. As would one of the city's thousands of taxis. But Nicky wanted to take him. What she *didn't* want was Flint criticizing her for trying to run his life again.

"Driving myself would probably be best," he agreed. "That way, you won't be coming home alone."

"Coming home alone at night isn't exactly unusual for me."

"It's not the hour but the circumstances—"

"Stop. Please." Before he spoiled her optimistic mood. She tamped down the renewal of irritation that quickly welled inside her. He did have reason to worry. "Even you can't believe those thugs would lie in wait for me in my own neighborhood," she said reasonably. "Besides, I'm not going to stop living because of what *might* happen."

He deliberated for a moment, then said, "Your meeting Dr. Galloway might not be a bad thing...considering what happened the other night."

Her pulse picked up a beat. Flint wanted her to go as well. Happy as that made her, Nicky tried to keep the situation in perspective.

"What time did Dr. Galloway tell you to show up?"

"Nine. And I'm supposed to be armed with toothbrush and pajamas."

"I already armed you with a spare toothbrush. As for the pajamas..." Remembering some of the more intimate details of his first night at her place, Nicky flushed. "...I guess you'll have to sleep in the ones you were born in...as usual."

To cover the discomfort her needling him caused, she threw a handful of newly fallen snow at Scraps. The dog was in a feisty mood after being penned in for so long, so she let him chase her and run circles around her all the way to the front door. About to go inside, she paused, a smile twitching at her lips. She gathered more of the white stuff, this time shaping it into a loosely-packed ball, which she pitched at Flint.

"Catch!" she called out, knowing it was already too late for him to duck.

He jerked at the hit. The missile left him with a dusting of white atop his dark hair.

Nicky snickered. "You make a pretty spiffy-looking senior citizen, Armstrong."

"You asked for it!" Flint growled, ducking to scoop up snow with both hands.

Scraps barked, indicating he wanted to join in the fun. Laughing, Nicky let the dog race over to Flint as she put the vestibule door between her and the snowball that thudded harmlessly against the glass. As he came inside, Scraps dancing at his heels, a grinning Flint brushed the remaining white flakes out of his hair.

"I owe you one," he warned her.

She said, "I'll be watching my back," then thought about the incident with the gang members. Gaze pinned to his jacket pocket, she asked, "By the way, when did you start carrying a weapon?"

"You mean this?"

Sticking his hand inside, he pulled out a dog toy and sent the mutt scrambling up the steps after it.

Nicky's heart almost stopped. "You were bluffing." He could have been hurt—maybe killed—if he hadn't been so good at it.

"I was raised in the inner city, remember."

She started up the stairs. "You were part of a gang?"

"No, which meant I had to be twice as tough to survive. I took my knocks."

"Who would have guessed?" Nicky murmured, hurrying to the landing.

Amazing that she could learn new things about Flint after all these years. It was almost as if she'd never known exactly who he was before.

Flint waited until she'd unlocked her door and they entered her apartment before asking, "Did you get any hint of what they wanted?"

"Me," she said. "You heard the leader say they were being paid. Someone sent them after me...undoubtedly Hector Villada."

"Not necessarily."

"Who else?"

"If you'll remember, I was answering the phone when you left. It was Cecilia, by the way. She was thrilled to hear my voice," he said sarcastically. "I hung up in time to see you load the dog into your car. But when I got outside, you were gone...and a silver Buick was turning the corner."

Remembering that she'd noticed the vehicle again on the way to her own car, Nicky wondered how she hadn't realized that it was following her. Then, again, she had been distracted by her own anger and anxiety.

"Why would a reporter want me hurt?" she murmured. "Even some scumbag reporter?"

"How do you know who's driving that car?"

"I guess I just assumed...who else?"

"Someone who doesn't like you poking your nose in his business."

"Eric Jensen?" The only other obvious choice, Nicky figured. "It's not like I've been asking all around town about him. Does he drive a silver Buick?"

"Beats me. But we can find out tomorrow by accessing records from the Department of Motor Vehicles."

Nicky grew thoughtful. The attack on her had seemed to have a logical source in Hector Villada.

Now she wasn't so certain. What if Flint was right about her stirring someone up?

What if she'd managed to spook the killer into coming after *her?*

FLINT REGRETTED his selfishness all the way to Lakeshore Medical Center. He didn't need handholding...and Nicky needed to be safe. So why hadn't he been able to resist her logic and insist on coming alone?

Why was he finding it so hard to resist *her?*

That nagged at him as they left the parking lot for the corridors of the medical facility. Nicky was quickly becoming an integral part of his life. Rather, she had become his emotional lifeline. Dealing with her was forcing him back to himself. He could feel the change inside, one that had started subtly but was quickly taking on a life of its own if his response to her being in danger earlier was any indication. He suspected the metamorphosis back to his old self would be complete if he hung around with Nicky long enough.

So was it gratitude added to years of affection that he felt for her? Or was he wading in far deeper than made him comfortable?

Not wanting to dissect the enigma now, he was relieved when they entered the sleep disorder center and he had to face the welcoming beam of the receptionist, who appeared a bit too perky for the late hour.

A night person, no doubt.

"You must be Mr. Armstrong and you Ms. Keating," she chirped, bouncing up from her desk. "Dr. Galloway said to bring you both right into her office the moment you arrived."

Flint had called ahead. Indeed, the psychotherapist had expressed interest in meeting the one person who'd witnessed his problem firsthand...and was still alive to tell the tale.

Oddly enough, upon entering the interior office, Nicky seemed a little nervous, unlike her normal self. After Flint made the introductions, she sat quietly rather than diving right in.

"I'm glad you agreed to come, Miss Keating," Dr. Galloway said. "If you can stay for a few minutes after we put Mr. Armstrong to bed, I'd like to talk to you about what happened the other night."

"Of course." Seeming hesitant, Nicky asked, "Is this problem...nightmares compounded by sleepwalking and violent episodes...common?"

"Actually, you're talking about two separate issues. Nightmares themselves are predictable and normal for someone who survived a disaster such as an earthquake. They're a typical response to events beyond our control. When we talk about dreams or nightmares we mean what goes on during REM or rapid eye movement sleep. The heart beats faster, the breathing quickens...the body muscles relax. It's like a safety mechanism in our brain that disconnects motor functions so we *can't* act out our dreams. This happens several times during the night, each period getting longer than the last, each dream becoming more complex. The person can usually remember the dream if he or she taps into it immediately upon awakening."

"But when the scary stuff happens," Nicky said, "Flint doesn't remember dreaming about anything."

"I've tried," Flint insisted. "All I come up with is an image, maybe a sound...."

"What you're describing happens during non-REM

or nonrapid eye movement sleep,'' Dr. Galloway continued. "This is normally the time when our brain waves are quiet. But in what's called night terrors or sleep terrors—a common problem although usually confined to childhood—and in sleepwalking in the adult, something goes awry. Something terrifies the sufferer into fleeing his bed to escape. Perhaps a recounting of the experienced trauma itself—because the person can't remember upon awakening, we don't really have any way of knowing for certain. Unfortunately, while in this state, the sufferer may often commit an act of violence to himself...or to someone else."

"Who happens to be in the wrong place at the wrong time," Flint said, thinking of Beverly.

"And you can prove this is what's happening to Flint?" Nicky asked.

"That's what we're hoping to do..." Dr. Galloway checked her watch "...right now, as a matter of fact." She rose and indicated they should both follow, continuing to talk as they left her office. "Normally, we shift between non-REM and REM sleep every ninety minutes or so, averaging two hours in REM every night. When this pattern is disturbed, the person becomes increasingly tired and tries to make up for it during subsequent sleep sessions. Several nights of continuing disturbances and the person can become a basket case."

"That explains a lot," Nicky murmured, as they walked down the corridor to the lab.

Indeed, Flint thought, after each frightening episode, he'd found that falling asleep would be difficult for days. He could recall several times when he'd felt like a zombie—walking around supposedly awake, while having difficulty dealing with the simplest tasks.

Somehow—Nicky's influence, no doubt—he'd fallen into a deep, healing sleep the night before, even after being tied to the bed and turned on by their teasing and her very sobering presence.

He could still feel her body whisking against his as she'd tied his wrist to the headboard....

"Here we are," Dr. Galloway said, snapping him back to his current circumstance.

They entered a lab area filled with electronic equipment, appearing to open off it was a half-dozen smaller rooms. A full-figured African-American woman entered through one of those doorways.

"Ah, there you are."

The psychotherapist made introductions. "Dana King is our top technician. She'll be overseeing your sleep sessions."

"Mr. Armstrong." Dana held out a hand with amazing nails—long and painted in intricate designs. "Let me show you to your quarters for the night."

Impressed by her firm grip—assuming he was being left in the best of hands—he told Nicky, "I'll see you in the morning."

She flashed him two thumbs up. "Bright and early."

Dana showed him into the private bedroom she'd just left. "I'll leave you alone for a few minutes so you can get ready for bed."

"No need. No pajamas." Flint pulled his sweater over his head. "I'm ready if you are."

"Then make yourself comfortable."

Sitting at the edge of the bed, he removed his boots. Then he stretched out. He tried to remain relaxed while Dana taped small electrodes at various places on his scalp, behind both ears, next to each eye and beneath his chin, but his muscles defied him, stiffening uncooperatively.

"The electrodes pick up signals from you and transmit them to the room next door," she explained as she worked. "Polygraph devices amplify the signals. All night, your brain waves, muscle changes and eye movements will be traced across a moving paper—a record of your sleep patterns. I'll also be keeping an eye on you through a video monitor."

The camera stared at him unblinking from a high corner of the room. There was nothing less natural than feeling like a lab specimen.

"And I'm supposed to fall asleep hot-wired and knowing I'm your evening's entertainment?"

Dana grinned. "Oh, maybe not at first. But you'll fall asleep eventually. Our clients always do in the absence of outside stimuli."

"So I sleep," he said, unconvinced, "while you watch. That's all there is to it?"

"It's a little more complicated, but that's the general idea. I'll be waking you at various times during the night. You'll hear your name over the intercom." She pointed out the speaker set near the head of the bed. "I'll ask you to tell me whatever's been going through your mind—any thoughts or dreams."

"What if I don't have anything to report?"

"Then that's what you'll tell me."

"That happens?"

"Everything or nothing could happen, Mr. Armstrong. I've seen and heard it all. Try to relax. Good night and...I was going to say pleasant dreams, but that's not exactly what you're here for now, is it?"

Leaving the room, she switched out the light.

Flint purposefully closed his eyes and concentrated on letting himself drift as a prelude to sleep, but his mind wouldn't cooperate. Wouldn't shut down. He expended an undetermined amount of effort before giving up and letting his thoughts wander where they would—straight back to the source of his downward spiral.

Like a televised year-end review, images flashed through his consciousness, starting with the earthquake. Not that he wanted to, he remembered everything.

Waking with the building folding down around him.
Finding Alana.
Entering Megan's room.
He couldn't stay there. Wouldn't.
Had to move on.

Flashes of the funeral taunted him. The move back to Chicago and the home he'd once shared with his wife and child. His trying to piece back together a life he'd thought he no longer wanted.

His trying to isolate himself.

Then Nicky was bullying him... Scraps idolizing him... Beverly accepting him.

Beverly dead.
Nicky in danger.

Nicky. She filled his head. Filled his heart. He'd been afraid for her earlier. No, terrified. He hadn't stopped to think before acting. He'd gone on automatic pilot when he'd placed himself between her and danger.

He'd been the one to place her in such jeopardy, Flint realized.

From the unknown.

From him.

She didn't deserve this. Not any of it. Certainly not him. She deserved a life of her own with a man who wanted nothing more than to make her happy. To take care of her.

Nicky with another man...

The thought nearly drove Flint crazy.

He couldn't forget holding her. Touching her. Kissing her.

Nor could he forget how she'd broken the connection. Afraid. Of him.

She had a right to be afraid, he reminded himself, for he was capable of anything, except maybe of stopping himself from wanting her.

How this had happened, Flint couldn't say. Nicky had been like his kid sister...then suddenly he was feeling more for her than he ever had for Beverly. Maybe more than he had for Alana...

Another reason to feel guilty?

Alana was dead, a voice inside him whispered. And he was alive. And he would never be able think of Nicky as a kid sister again.

Chapter Nine

Nicky left Dr. Galloway's office nearly an hour later, following some frank talk about the chances of getting the results they wanted on the first try. The psychotherapist had warned her not to be too optimistic.

And yet...

Not only was Flint due for a break, he was finally ready for one if she were any judge.

Nicky kept that positive fact uppermost in mind as she traversed the empty corridor that would take her to the parking garage.

Even separated from Flint, she somehow sensed the welcome return of a life force that she'd feared had been extinguished. She should have known how strong he really was, deep inside, where it counted. One traumatic loss might have smothered the flames of his spirit, but not so the embers of his soul. Too bad it had taken an equally horrible death—not to mention her prodding and poking—to jolt him back from the abyss. And even so, she knew his footing was still tenuous.

Should Flint be convicted of murder...

Arriving at the hallway housing the garage elevator,

Nicky punched the call button with extra force and vowed not to consider such negativity.

She had to stop morbid thoughts from getting to her. Even now, in a public place—albeit a very deserted one—she found herself a little spooked. From the way the hair on the back of her arms stood at attention, she could almost believe someone was watching her.

Of course…security.

Assuming she was under electronic surveillance, she looked overhead. No candid camera that she could spot. And yet the sensation of being watched intensified. She shifted. Turned around. Checked the area behind her. Wished for some other pedestrian she could put a face to.

No one.

Back to the elevator…what was taking so long?

What if…?

Heat suddenly flushed up Nicky's neck, while sweat prickled her skin. Inside, she felt as if she had an itch she couldn't scratch. Nerves. She hit the lit call button a few more times for good measure, then strained to hear beyond the faint sounds of a medical cart moving down some nearby hallway. No car speeding its way to her along its shaft. No electrical bells and whistles.

Nothing.

Someone must have stopped the darned elevator on another floor.

Antsy, Nicky decided there was no use in waiting even if the door to the nearby stairs was marked Emergency Exit Only. As far as she was concerned, her not being able to get to her vehicle at will constituted an emergency. So she popped open the steel door and stepped into a cold, gray stairwell.

Glaring light from uncovered bulbs blasted each

landing, steps between falling prey to dark shadows. When she began her descent, Nicky listened to her footsteps echo eerily up and around the Spartan concrete and steel chamber. There could be two of her, she thought, sounds pounding at her until she was confused, left wondering if she really did hear a second set. Try as she might, she couldn't tell whether she was truly alone.

Her imagination spurred her downward even faster, the reverberating footfalls following with equal rapidity. The cadence mimicked the blood rushing through her head and the rasp of her breath wheezing through her throat.

After bursting through the door to Parking Level 3, she stopped cold for a moment. Having used a different means of entry than before, she wasn't sure of her direction. Sides open to the elements, the facility provided little more amenity than a protective roof with a few inadequate lights marking ramps and exits.

Orienting herself, she started off to the right, her focus split between the sea of cars before her and the area behind that had been swallowed by shadows, from which came scrabbling sounds.

The garage itself seemed to be alive.

Breathing.

Laughing at her.

Finally spotting the Escort several rows over, Nicky took a long swallow of cold air and told herself to get a grip. It was then that the sudden absence of sound struck her with its significance. Good grief, she'd been tuning in to the raggedness of her own breath!

What a goof!

Feeling foolish, she cut between two minivans, her pulse settling, her whole body sagging with relief.

And then a blazing light suddenly blinded her.

Nicky yipped and backed up.

A hulking shadow at the light's source blocked her way, growling, "Stop right there!"

"Don't try anything or you'll be s-sorry!" she sputtered, praying she could find the energy to put up a fight.

"You're the one who's gonna be sorry, lady, unless you got a good reason for using the emergency exit and bringing me running!"

Her "What?" sounded strangled to her own ears.

The light flashed on the man's uniform. "Security."

"Oh." Laughter bubbled from her throat. "Oh, dear!"

Once started, she couldn't stop laughing. She *had* been chased—by a security guard of all people. What could be more ironic?

"You a wiseacre?"

"No...really...you scared me is all. I thought..." Catching her breath, she tried to explain. "The elevator wasn't coming so I decided to walk down."

"And set off an alarm in the security office," the guy muttered in disgust. He backed off, opening the way for her. "All right. Get going."

"Thanks," she said, somehow moving forward when all her muscles felt about as solid as cooked spaghetti. "And thanks for coming to my rescue...even though I didn't actually need one."

Even though *he* had scared her into thinking she did.

"Yeah, yeah, yeah," the man groused as he ambled off.

Drained, Nicky unlocked her car and slid behind the driver's seat, immediately securing her door. No sense in taking chances. For a moment, she sat there, head back against the rest, waiting for her vital signs to right. Then she started the engine. The warmth of her breath was already screwing up visibility, so she turned on the defrosters.

The windshield...

Eyes widening, she stared as the plate of glass before her fogged up, leaving a deliberate if crude pattern drawn on the *inside.*

A fact that shook her to her core.

Trembling, she checked the back seat and locks but found nothing to indicate that anyone had broken in. Yet the drawing on her windshield proved otherwise.

The scales of justice overlaid with a circle and a slash.

Nicky got the indirect but clear message.

Someone didn't want her interfering...

As angry as she was scared, she rolled down her side window and yelled, "You can't stop me, you coward!" then expected the prompt return of the security guard.

But the only audible response was more scrabbling noises from the shadows...while the rising heat from the dash obliterated the warning on the windshield...

Nicky's mind raced faster than her vehicle as she sped out of the garage, her gaze scanning the rows of parked cars for sight of a familiar figure.

Or a silver Buick.

But the winter's night yielded no answers. No clues. No indication that anything was wrong.

Tense all the way home, Nicky was paranoid by the time she had to park again. Thankfully, a spot almost directly opposite her front door awaited. Then, keys in hand, she flew to the vestibule and let herself inside, fumbling with the downstairs lock. Even when that door lay between her and anyone who might be following, she couldn't relax.

Who was to say that the person who got into her car couldn't have done the same to her apartment?

Couldn't be waiting for her even now?

She took the stairs with caution, nearly nauseated with the effort to stay calm as she approached her own door.

Ear against the wood, she whispered, "Scraps," and heard a normal snuffling in return.

Forehead bowed in thanks, she went inside, quickly bolting the door behind her, then nearly jumping out of her skin as the phone chose that moment to shatter the silence.

She glanced at her watch. Nearly eleven. Who would call her so late?

Hopefully, her mother.

With the dog at her side, she picked up on the third ring. "Hello?"

Silence.

Her fingers tightened around the receiver. "Hello?"

Someone was there. Not answering.

Under no illusion now that this might be a reporter, Nicky waited, heart in her throat, anger quickly resurfacing. Though she'd have liked to play the same game, she couldn't keep silent.

"Justice isn't always blind," she told the person who most certainly had left her the cryptic message on the windshield. Her voice was tight but seemingly calm. "And it can catch up with you when you least expect—"

Click.

With some sense of satisfaction, she hung up, then noticed the blinking light on her answering machine.

According to the counter, she'd had eleven calls in the past three hours. Certain of what she'd find, she played back her messages anyway.

Every one of them blank.

Leaving her not a shred of proof...no more than could be found on her windshield...as if nothing had happened...nothing, at all...

"NOTHING, HUH?" Nicky mumbled, trying to contain her disappointment when Flint declared the laboratory sleep session to have been a failure.

Another negative emotion added to the one she was already experiencing merely by returning to the medical center. At least she'd been able to find parking on the street a few blocks' walk away.

"I did warn you." Ensconced behind her office desk, Dr. Galloway reminded her of the private conversation they'd had the night before, after Flint had been turned over to the technician. "Trying for *normal* in a laboratory where the sleeper is being watched and evaluated obviously has disadvantages that are bound to prejudice dream reports."

"But I didn't dream—or sleep—at all."

Nicky worriedly gazed at Flint, who'd regained the pallor of exhaustion. She believed him, though the psychotherapist was shaking her head.

"Actually, that's not exactly true, Mr. Armstrong. Perhaps you had little deep or REM sleep due to various anxieties, but your night was filled with non-REM time. Often our thoughts during these periods are so logical that we're certain we're awake and that our minds are going around and around with our problems. Many people who believe they're insomniacs really are sleeping, if lightly, and they're doing their contemplating in extended non-REM.''

"So then we *are* on the right track?" Nicky ventured, desperate to grasp onto something positive. Her experience the night before had shattered her outlook.

"Well, I wouldn't be discouraged because nothing in the way of sleepwalking took place."

A statement that didn't reassure her. Or Flint.

He muttered, "Meaning we're still at square one."

"For the moment," Dr. Galloway agreed. "But I've already told you we don't give up after one disappointment. Think of tonight as a new opportunity."

"Or another shot at nothing," he groused.

Neither woman commented. Nicky wondered which was making Flint grouchier—the actual lack of sleep or the lack of proof that he had a definable, hopefully solvable problem. Convinced he was finally reaching for the helping hand others were offering, she suspected the latter.

"I didn't get much sleep myself," she admitted, not that she was about to tell him why.

What Flint didn't know wouldn't hurt him. Who could tell what damaging effect her telling him might have? Nothing had actually happened to her anyway, Nicky reassured herself. She'd only gotten a good scare.

If only she could figure out how the person had gotten into her car without leaving a trace. Surely any burglar tool would leave marks of some kind.

A phantom burglar...phantom murderer...were they interchangeable?

"We'll try again tonight," Dr. Galloway was saying. "Same time, same place?"

Flint rose, agreeing. "I'll be back."

"It's a date, then."

Nicky knew it was rare for Dr. Galloway to spend the night in the lab these days. The psychotherapist had admitted her responsibilities as an administrator in a growing field took up so much of her time that she was rarely able to indulge in the hands-on work that had been her first love. But obviously, the outcome of Flint's circumstance was of enough significance that she was willing to do double duty.

Grateful, Nicky gave Dr. Galloway a tremulous smile before leaving the office with Flint. She would think positively and continue to hope for the best. Now certain that Flint was actually innocent of having any part in Beverly's death, she knew it would still behoove them to have the psychotherapist's backing for a legal defense.

Just in case...

They were halfway to the car before Flint asked, "So what's on the agenda for the day?"

Nicky narrowed her gaze at him. "Aren't you being a little too agreeable?"

"I thought you wanted me to cooperate."

"I do."

"Well, then?"

Still suspicious, she checked her watch. "I don't think the ACT offices would be open yet. Besides, you look like you could use an energy boost."

"You're hungry."

Though she'd hardly had time to walk the dog that morning, all she would admit to was "I could use a cup of coffee."

"And a few tasty things to wash down with it," Flint said.

Amazed at his tractable mood considering his unsuccessful night, Nicky chose not to fight it. Stopping at a family restaurant on the way downtown, she let Flint buy her a substantial breakfast, after which she coerced him into walking the rest of the way so the calories didn't have a chance to collect around her hips. She figured she would have to start improvising if she didn't want her fitness level to backslide. And the exercise was actually a plus for Flint. Within blocks, he literally appeared revitalized.

"So what did you do with yourself last night?" he asked.

Nicky started guiltily, then quickly told herself he couldn't possibly guess....

Doing her best to act natural so she wouldn't give it away, she asked, "What makes you think I did anything but go home and go to bed?"

"You said you didn't get much sleep."

"Worrying about you." It was partly true.

Flint seemed worried about *her* when he said, "You shouldn't."

Or was it that her too-personal interest was making him uncomfortable? Nicky wondered, remembering his negative response to her following their kiss.

Was this a delicate of way of asking her to back off?

"I can't make myself stop, Flint," she said honestly, concentrating on the intersection so she wouldn't have to look him in the eye. She couldn't stop caring about him. "I don't know anyone with that kind of control. Not even you." Before he could argue the point, she changed the subject. "Anyhow, I made plans for tonight with Mom."

Whom she'd called to make herself feel better after being so spooked.

"Well. Cecilia certainly is finding time for you these days."

Unable to miss the irony in his tone, Nicky flushed. Anyone who wasn't blind, deaf and dumb knew Cecilia Keating had preferred her older daughter's company when given the choice. She hadn't forgotten her worry that her mother—and he—saw her as an Alana substitute.

"We're getting closer," she insisted, trying to convince herself as well as him.

Her mother had sounded so concerned about her without being judgmental, that Nicky had even owned up to her activities—some of them, anyway—in trying to clear Flint's name. She'd been gratified *not* to hear criticism for once.

"If that's true," Flint was saying, "I'm happy for you."

Considering the long-term animosity between the two people she cared most about, Nicky was happy that Flint could find it in himself to be so generous.

"Tonight should be fun, listening to some blues together," she said with true enthusiasm. Music had always been important to her mother. "Mom's new friend, Oren Maticek, is the owner of a small club called Listen to the Night." And at last she'd get to meet him. "I'm joining her there right after I drop you off at the center."

"I am able to get around on my own. You don't have to feel obligated—"

"I do things because I want to."

And because she refused to let some phantom miscreant scare her off.

Arriving at the building that housed ACT Legal

Support Team, they were in for an unpleasant surprise. Two men blocked their entry into the building.

A slickly dressed, fair-haired man identified himself. "Rod Hanover, *National Investigator*." And held out a palm-sized recorder.

His sidekick began snapping photographs immediately. Nicky ducked her head and tried to shoulder her way around the men, but they effectively kept her from going inside.

"Get out of our way," Flint said tightly, placing himself between her and them.

"Or what?" Hanover asked. "You can't have us arrested. What are you gonna do? Take us to the cleaners in court like you did Sid Shelton?"

Nicky started. Why would he bring up Shelton? How would he even have found out about the car parts dealer? Had Shelton spoken to him?

Flint calmly said, "A client sued him, not me."

"But you were highly aggressive in pursuing information to use against him."

"I was doing my job."

"Like I'm only doing *my* job," the reporter returned. "So how about giving me something on that sleep center you spent the night at?"

Nicky felt Flint stiffen. Her own buttons were pushed, big time. She couldn't believe the wretched reporter had been able to find out about the center to begin with. Unless, of course, he had followed her...

Popping out from behind Flint, she demanded to know, "What kind of a car do you drive?"

"Huh? Toyota. Why?"

"What about you?" she asked the photographer.

The homely face revealed by the lowered camera appeared puzzled. "Is this some kinda test?"

"Your car?" she pressed.

"A Camaro. Vintage."

"Not them," Flint said with a shrug.

And before they could recoup, he pushed between them, sweeping Nicky along with him. Luckily they got into an elevator before the team caught up to them.

"Do you believe they knew..." Aware of other people in the car, Nicky finished, "about those things?"

"Doesn't really surprise me."

Nicky realized she must be feeling more upset than Flint was acting, but she shelved the discussion for later and turned her mind to the work at hand.

Neither partner was in yet, so Sher ushered them into Terrence's inner sanctum, saying, "If I can do anything...keep it to yourself until after nine, would you? I'm expecting an important phone call any minute now."

Eyes widening at the woman's temerity in being so frank about her personal problems at work, Nicky said, "Keeping him waiting wouldn't hurt."

"What I have to say to *this* creep won't keep." Sher straightened her spine as she waltzed back out the door. "He's not shipping our supply orders on time."

Flint was grinning. "I'd hate to be on the other end of that conversation."

Nicky laughed at her own assumption. "It sounds like she has things in hand around here."

First on the agenda was checking out the Department of Motor Vehicle records for a newer-model silver Buick. Flint showed her what to do, then let her take over. Aware of him watching her, she was a little self-conscious, but he didn't comment when she faltered, and she appreciated that he patiently waited for her to work things through rather than jump to her assistance. Nicky had to admit to a fascination with finding bits of information that, when put together, could tell a story.

"Don't you miss this kind of digging?" she asked him.

"I never stopped. I could be working this moment."

Right. Temporary work with a collections agency.

"Tracking down people with delinquent charge accounts or hospital bills isn't exactly the same thing," Nicky suggested, trying to maintain some subtlety.

"It's a living."

"One that you care about?"

"I hate it mostly," Flint admitted. "The part about tracking down the little guy, that is. Who am I to add to someone else's burden in life?"

Certain that unpleasantness didn't help his dark moods, she said, "So do something else."

"Work on commercial accounts isn't always available."

"That's not what I meant."

"What, then?" Leaning forward, he indicated the file she was searching. "This?"

"Why not?"

Aware of how close he'd gotten, Nicky had some difficulty keeping her mind where she'd aimed it. Resisting Flint's effect on her, she tried to concentrate on continuing the no-pressure pep talk. She'd been holding back for far too long, lest she get more flak from him and turn him off for good. But things were changing, and she felt now was the time for a little support. Doing something meaningful—whether helping to incarcerate the bad guys or free the innocent—was bound to give Flint renewed satisfaction in life.

"At lunch yesterday," she continued, entering a few more keystrokes, "I'm pretty sure Linda was fishing around with those stories about tough cases to see if you were interested."

"I don't need a pity job."

"I don't think pity was what she had in... " The screen changed and Nicky let the statement trail off as she focused on the information. "Hello, Eric Jensen. Let's see what kind of baby you drive." But a few more keystrokes brought her only disappointment. "Hmm. This lists him as having two cars, both imports."

"So much for that idea."

Used to being denied instant gratification, she wasn't prepared to give up. "What about Sid Shelton?"

"Shelton? You think he's a possible?" Flint mused, forehead pulling into a frown.

She couldn't help but be fascinated by the way the scar that slashed through his eyebrow knitted together. "I think he's a viable suspect."

"When was it you first noticed the Buick?"

"After he accosted you..." She pulled her gaze back to the monitor. "Later that day."

"Not exactly a lot of time to investigate you."

"Who's to say he didn't already have his antennae out?" Nicky suggested, typing in the car parts dealer's name. "We were splashed all over the morning tabloids. And are you forgetting he didn't have a reason to be at Twenty-Sixth and California other than to harass you? I wouldn't presume to guess what kind of information he's gathered together, not only about you and me, but about anyone else you know.''

"So give it a whirl."

"I already have." The field before her eyes stabilized, allowing her to scan the screen. "Nope. He drives American. The competition. Officially, anyhow. From what you've told me, he undoubtedly has any brand of vehicle he chooses at his disposal."

"Not that he keeps records on those cars."

Impulsively, Nicky said, "I could use a nice long drive around the city. What about you?"

"Where to?"

"Wherever we might find Sid Shelton."

"Shelton?" The echo came from the doorway. "What's *he* got to do with anything?"

She turned to see Terrence entering his office, surprise etched on his narrow face.

"Such fortuitous timing," she murmured, quickly explaining what they were about.

Seeming happy to give them whatever he could on Sid Shelton, Terrence dug into a file drawer behind his desk and pulled out a folder that he handed to Flint.

"About six months ago, we were in the process of gathering information for another lawsuit against this scum when the client canceled." He punched his titanium glassed frames into place at the bridge of his nose. "I suspect they struck some kind of deal. I don't even know what in here is valid anymore—I hired someone else to do the legwork—but you're welcome to whatever you can find."

Sorting out documents, Flint copied down a few addresses.

"Two of these are familiar," he said, pausing to

study a handwritten note. "This one on the west side doesn't ring a bell."

"Probably a new location to take advantage of the United Center crowd," Terrence said.

Which Nicky took to mean Shelton might have a chop shop near the new sports complex, though she didn't see how car thieves could be successful with the improved security of high fences and electronic monitors, not to mention extra guards. Then, again, she guessed career criminals grew more sophisticated with the nature of the challenge.

Because Terrence insisted he had some free time he didn't want to waste, Flint accepted his offer of help. After going over the little they knew about their three suspects, Terrence volunteered to canvass Logan Square in search of Hector Villada.

"Dressed like that?" Flint asked, expression skeptical as he took in his ex-partner's tailored appearance.

"You know me better than that, my man. I can still pass for a homie if I gotta," he insisted.

Making Nicky wonder about his roots. Undoubtedly he'd been an inner city kid like Flint. Remembering their experience the day before, she only hoped he was equally tough.

Once Terrence left, Flint took over for a while and ran a check on Shelton's business licenses. None listed at the west-side address that he could find.

"I guess we'll have to see what's there for ourselves," Nicky said.

"Not we. *Me*."

His tone put her on alert. "Getting macho?"

"Getting smart. I'll be safer if you're not around."

"A blatant attempt to play on my conscience," she said, wondering if it wasn't actually the truth. He could have been in hot water, big time, with those gang members. Then, again, if she wasn't with him, who would watch *his* back? "Which I'll happily ignore this once."

"Nicky…"

She bristled at his warning tone. "Don't *Nicky* me." And to distract him from his purpose, she added, "While we're out, we should pay Eric Jensen a visit, as well."

"To what end?"

"To see if we can spook him."

Even as Jensen might have spooked *her* the night before. Fair was fair.

If only the telephone company and police department had their acts together. She'd thought to make a formal complaint about being harassed so she could get the number—and therefore the identity—of her caller.

She'd learned she could after a fashion.

By dialing a code, she would make a complaint, automatically sending the caller's number into some data bank. Then she'd have to follow up with the police to obtain the information. The trick was…not for *five days*. And she'd have to pay for the service, to boot.

Five days. And they called this the information age!

One way or another, Nicky figured, she and Flint would find the phantom bastard who'd spooked her faster themselves.

Chapter Ten

Not really seeing the point in paying Jensen a visit, Flint nevertheless refrained from offering that opinion. After picking up Nicky's car where they'd left it earlier, they made for E.J. Contractors, which was on the way to the west-side address. Located on a side street beyond River North, the small storefront office was crowded, every horizontal surface supporting plumbing and heating supplies.

"Eric's on site this morning," the office manager told them, her fine brow furrowed as she stared as if trying to place his face.

"Where would that be?" he asked.

Nicky was looking over a wall calendar as the other woman said, "At a school. I can page him—"

"Not necessary. But you *can* let him know we stopped by."

"What did you say your name was?" the office manager asked, pen poised over a message pad.

"Armstrong. Tell him Flint Armstrong stopped by to see him."

She gaped. "I thought—" Then abruptly clamped her mouth shut.

Flint turned to Nicky, who was trying to be covert

about her interest in the scheduling calendar. Tucking his hand in the crook of her arm, he pushed her toward the door.

She waited until they were outside before saying, "I got the location. Alvarez School, about a mile from here."

"Maybe we should swing by to see what kind of vehicles are parked out front."

Once they were on their way, Nicky said, "So a person with an uncontrollable temper and a police record of physical abuse gets to work around impressionable kids. Swell. According to the calendar, E.J. Contractors is servicing several public schools even after we're back in session."

"His civil right." One of those kinks in the justice system that reminded Flint it wasn't perfect. Because Nicky was a teacher, he suspected she had strong feelings on this particular subject. "Beverly mentioned her ex-husband bid on contracts for all kinds of government facilities. She used to give him a hand when she could until she heard a couple of complaints about his utilizing substandard materials."

"When was that?"

"She didn't say."

A nebulous bit of information that he hadn't before considered, yet enough to make him wonder if the situation was more serious than Beverly had indicated. What if Jensen had been scamming government agencies and, as a prosecutor, Beverly had felt obliged to do something about it?

Nicky's inclination to imagine motives for other people seemed to be catching....

"This is the block," she said, slowing. "Start keeping an eye out for the car."

But the moment they pulled within sight of Alvarez School, Eric Jensen flew out the front door and headed them off.

Nicky stepped on the brakes and muttered, "Uh-oh. She warned him."

And with a sense of fatality, Flint left the car. "Stay put," he warned her, hoping for once she would listen to him. Pumped despite himself, he slammed the door and turned to the man whose rage seemed ready to spill over on him.

"What are you doing here, Armstrong?"

"Taking a drive, Jensen. Touring the neighborhood."

"Harassing me?"

Flint kept his cool. "A compliment coming from the harassment expert."

"Don't mess with me—"

"Or you'll what? Get an injunction against me? We all know how well those work." Gaze steady, he was gratified when color flushed the other man's face. And he couldn't resist asking, "How's business?"

For a moment, Jensen appeared apoplectic. Then he demanded, "What the bloody blue blazes are you up to?"

And Flint realized he'd pushed some sensitive button. He kept going. "Just wondering if you got things straightened out."

"What things?"

"It isn't as easy to mess around with a government contract as it used to be." Without specifics, he was on a fishing expedition. "The little people get upset when their tax money is misspent on substandard goods."

"Where do you get your information?"

"Beverly." Without considering what he was doing, Flint kept at Jensen. "Until someone made sure she couldn't tell me what she knew anymore."

"If you're intimating *I* had anything to do with her death, you've got a lot of nerve!" the other man yelled. "Bev died in *your* bed."

"Actually...not. She died in the dining room." Flint spoke tonelessly, as if his gut weren't knotted at the knowledge. He realized he was rediscovering his center. Regaining tools that he'd thought were lost forever. "Where did you say you were on Christmas Eve?"

"Not that it's any of your business, I happened to be at a charity fund-raiser given by a client. I have witnesses, Armstrong, so don't get any ideas about how you can pass on the blame to me."

"You also had motive. Maybe more than one. And if I do go to trial, Phelps Rendell will make certain you'll have some explaining to do whether you want to or not."

The man moved so fast that Flint almost didn't duck in time. The miss was a matter of centimeters. The other man's fist smashing into the car roof gratified him and kept him from retaliating in kind. Jensen swore, backed off and cradled his hand as Nicky flew across the seat and rolled down the passenger window.

"Hey, better watch it or I'll press charges for vehicular abuse!" she warned him.

Before Jensen could curse her, too, Flint asked, "What did you say the name of that client was?"

"Go to hell!" Whirling around, Jensen stalked back toward the school, slipping across a slick patch of smooth snow.

"Been there, done that," Flint called after him.

He'd been trapped in a living hell of guilt for nearly a year, but surprisingly, he could feel the bands loosening.... "We'll have to trade war stories."

Flint got back into the car and secured his seatbelt, extraordinarily satisfied at feeling so alive.

"I'd say you made *his* day," Nicky said, sounding impressed.

"And my own," he admitted, gratified yet again when she beamed at him.

Half-worried that she might start gushing, Flint was relieved when she merely drove off, head turning from side to side as she continued searching for the Buick. He kept on the lookout, as well. Maybe he was crazy, but the wild-goose chase they were on had suddenly become oddly appealing.

Almost any time he spent in Nicky's company was appealing, he admitted, unable to imagine what life would be like without her....

"You two were talking so loud, I got the gist of that alibi exchange," she said, taking the corner. "The fund-raiser was to provide housing for the homeless."

"How do you know that?"

"The production calendar in Jensen's office. I checked December 24. The company is River West Realty. Probably sponsoring some kind of building renovation, which, of course is Jensen's business."

"We can follow up on his alibi later." Flint noted they were on their way to the west side. "And while we're at it...his finances."

"You can do that? How?"

"No problem. Despite warnings about keeping our social security numbers protected so they can't be used in a credit card or other scam, an enterprising company is selling our numbers over the Internet. You have to request to be taken off the list in writing.''

''You're kidding.''

''Nope. And like you...and most other people...Jensen probably knows nothing about it. Once we have his social security number, we can open doors to his credit history and other financial information.''

Within minutes, they were in a fringe neighborhood of open lots and battered commercial venues interspersed between downtrodden two-and three-flats and a couple of public housing projects. They tracked down the address Flint had taken from Shelton's file to a corner warehouse covered with gang signs. To say the building looked neglected would be a compliment. In his opinion, the place should be razed.

Nicky pulled up to the curb and craned for a better look. ''I think it's deserted.''

''I'll check.''

But this time when he got out, she did, as well. Flint figured arguing would be useless.

The windows were boarded up. And on closer inspection, the main door was padlocked. Nicky was already rounding a corner, venturing into the alley.

''Loading dock area,'' she called to him.

Keeping an eye on their surroundings—mostly deserted but for a handful of younger kids—Flint caught up to her. No signs of life anywhere, though there had been once, if the awful smell of something rotting were any indication. Pretty bad, considering the cold weather and all.

''It's deserted, all right,'' he announced, taking shallow breaths. ''So we can leave.''

''Not so fast.'' Gripping the handle to a loading dock door, Nicky put her slight weight into it. Metal screeched in protest but the rusted panel slid open a couple of feet, enough for her to squeeze through. "C'mon."

"Nicky!"

Fearing for her safety, Flint moved fast to keep up with her. But nothing more sinister than rubble and shadows awaited them inside. Sunlight barely touched the place. The same went for the bare bulb that flicked on from a wall switch that surprised him when it worked.

Rusted metal car parts were gathered in piles along with pieces of the broken building itself. An uneasy Flint eyed a crooked support column and the sagging ceiling above and wondered how long the place had yet to stand.

A shudder ran through him, but he ignored the strange sensation and the fact that wandering around the decrepit structure set his stomach churning. Thankfully, they could get out of there. Though he might have been correct about the chop shop operation, it was clear that no one had used the place for quite a while.

"Either the police were on to Shelton, or the building was so dangerous that even he was afraid to use it. No point in our staying."

"Rats!"

He flashed to where Nicky was poking around. "Well, get away from there!"

"Huh?" Her puzzled expression cleared. "No, I didn't spot a furry beast," she said with a laugh. "I was just expressing my disappointment. I was hoping to find something helpful in nailing Shelton."

"As in?" When she shrugged, he said, "Truthfully,

I don't think the man has a subtle enough mind to set anyone up for murder in the first place.''

''But his being after *your* hide rather than Beverly's wouldn't be too subtle. And you're reminding me of your lawyer.'' She sounded disgusted. ''Refusing to check out Hector Villada because of preconceived notions on how a gang member would operate.''

''A point well-taken though.''

''Maybe.'' She stooped to pick up an object, which she inspected, then sent sailing. ''So, you don't think Shelton would resort to violence to get revenge?''

''Over money? Hard to believe, especially since I was merely instrumental, not the person who sued him. Besides, he obviously recouped his losses.''

''Why can't you let yourself go?'' Nicky asked, unzipping her jacket as if she were determined to stay until she found evidence of his innocence. ''Try to imagine you might not have killed anyone.''

''I have tried. Don't you think I would like to believe someone else is responsible? I'd give anything to know it wasn't me, accident or not.''

The dismal setting reminded him that he still had Alana and Megan on his conscience. No matter that Dr. Galloway had tried to ease his mind on that score.

No matter that Nicky had, as well...

''I know you didn't kill anyone.''

She sounded so certain of herself that Flint envied her. ''You're some cheerleader.''

''Cheerleader?'' She faked indignation. ''Hey, watch that! I'm the one who runs with the ball, remember?''

And she never stopped, never appeared defeated. Even now she was continuing to probe the dark recesses of the warehouse. She didn't know when to give up.

"You're a whole pep rally and game rolled into one. You're a truly competent and confident person."

"Not always." She moved from one pile to another, and bracing one hand against a support column, started toeing the loose debris until she uncovered what looked like part of a fallen beam. "I have my own insecurities."

Cecilia, Flint thought, growing uneasy as he watched the rubble unfold. "Through no fault of your own." In retrospect, her mother's ignoring her might have been the best thing that could have happened to Nicky. She could have turned out to be another Alana....

Still staring at the pile at her feet, he imagined her uncovering something pale...like flesh.

His chest tightened until a closer look proved the object to be nothing more menacing than old rags. But when she shifted her weight against the column, dirt sifted between them in a steady stream.

"Yikes!" She let go.

The building itself seemed to scream. Flint's head went light. Acting on pure instinct, he lunged forward and grabbed Nicky, whipping her toward the exit as the structure imploded around them.

She screeched and yelled, "What the heck do you think you're doing, Armstrong?"

Heart pounding, throat closed, he hesitated. The floor was solid beneath his feet. The walls standing. The ceiling intact. The noise echoing through his head fading.

He took a good look at Nicky, wide-eyed with fright, and realized he'd done that to her.

The building wasn't collapsing.

"Sorry. I didn't mean to…I had a flash…the earthquake."

Even now in his mind's eye, he could see the walls folding down on him, could hear the death scream of the apartment house. He ran a hand over his eyes…as if he could ever obliterate the memory.

"You're shaking." Immediately, she slipped comforting arms around his waist beneath his jacket. "It must have been so awful for you. To go through that alone…"

He could tell she wasn't looking for further explanation. Or any response. She was being Nicky. Accepting. Offering him comfort without rationalization because that was what she did and who she was.

Even if he'd wanted to, Flint couldn't have stopped himself from wrapping his arms around her shoulders and holding on to her. And he didn't want to.

What he wanted was to hang on to her…

Forever…

"Nicky…" he whispered.

He could feel her quickened heartbeat through her sweater. Her breath caught in her throat and her fingers dug into the flesh of his back. He tightened inside, the emotional reaction quickly prompting the physical.

Desire swamped him.

The urge to kiss her again…to touch her in every pleasurable way he knew how…to hold her in his arms until they both fell asleep…to be with her upon awakening.

He fought it. Fought himself. It wasn't going to happen. It couldn't.

He couldn't allow it.

If he kissed her...touched her...he would go mad with the wanting.

Because he *couldn't* subject her to such danger.

To him.

In the end, he let her go. "Sorry."

Expression peculiar, she nodded and looked toward the exit. "Maybe we should get out of here before something else happens."

Did she mean the building crashing around their ears?

Or between the two of them?

Flint didn't want to pursue this line of thought. He had too much emotional baggage to handle as it was.

Alana and Megan's ghosts...

Besides which, Nicky was undoubtedly feeling sorry for him. For her sister's widower.

They backtracked down the alley, but his mind lingered in the warehouse, dissecting the emotions Nicky continued to stir up. He put one foot in front of the other, distracted until she stumbled to a halt directly in front of him.

"Omigod! Look!" Before he could grasp what she meant, she started running. "The Buick!"

Catching a flash of silver cruising by at the intersection of alley and street, he yelled, "See if you can read the license plate!" then tore across the broken pavement to catch up.

They made the sidewalk nearly as one. Catching movement from the corner of his eye, Flint whirled around as a man wearing a grease-streaked blue parka disappeared between two buildings on the opposite side of the alley. He redirected his attention, but the Buick was already rounding the corner.

Nicky was puffing as she slowed. "L-T—"

"M," he said, a smear of dirty encrusted snow over the plate half-hiding the third letter.

"Are you sure...?" And as the car pulled out of view, she added, "There's a 2...something. Damn! A few more seconds and we'd have had the whole thing."

Flint committed the information to memory. "We can program the computer to list all owners whose licenses are variations grouped with those identifiers. Between us, maybe we'll recognize a name."

"How many possibilities would that make?"

"Three missing numbers...only nine-hundred and ninety-nine..."

"A thousand. Swell." She crossed her eyes. "That should keep us busy for a while. Oh, well, at least it's a start." She pulled her car keys from her pocket. "So, are you still counting out Shelton?"

"What should change my mind? The Buick's following us here?"

"That car wasn't following us or I would have spotted it," she insisted. "I was keeping an eye out the whole time."

"Then how do you explain its sudden appearance?"

"If the car belongs to one of Shelton's flunkies, the guy could have come by the warehouse to check on something. Simple coincidence. Accidents do happen."

"Sounds a little too convenient to me."

"Then what's your explanation?"

That was the problem, Flint admitted.

He didn't have one.

"NICOLE, THERE YOU ARE. I was beginning to wonder if you'd changed your mind about coming."

Ensconced in the middle of a raised booth at the front of the crowded club where Nicky had agreed to meet her, wearing a pale gold silk dress and her pearl choker, Cecilia Keating looked as if she were royalty waiting to be entertained. Indeed, the stage was, at the moment, unoccupied. Recorded soft jazz was being piped in through the sound system.

Though her mother knew perfectly well that she'd intended to drop Flint off at the medical center first, Nicky chose not to take exception. "I'm here now."

"And I'm so glad. You look very nice tonight."

Having taken extra care to pick a dress that would get her mother's approval—a plain dark green jersey accented with a chrome and brass pin—Nicky was pleased. She bent over to kiss her mother's cheek and received a big hug and kiss in return. She was grinning when she slid into the booth that the older woman occupied alone.

"So where's your friend?"

"Oren's around. Being the owner and all, he needs to keep on top of things. He's anxious to meet you, as well."

Nicky had never heard her mother sound so enthusiastic about a suitor before. And she appeared radiant, happiness and the low romantic lighting removing a decade from her already young-looking features.

"I'm glad things are going smoothly for you two."

"Yes, Oren is working out quite nicely. Even better than I had hoped."

Which made it sound more like business than romance, Nicky thought. But that had always been her mother's way—people having to prove themselves to her over and over. She guessed it came from an innate insecurity that must have started in childhood and that had definitely been exacerbated by Nicky's father when he'd walked out on his family.

How could any woman who'd gone through such a stressful situation not become hypercritical of a man's every move until she was sure of him?

A waitress wearing an elegant cocktail dress took drink orders. Nicky went with her mother's favorite, a Kir Royale, champagne kissed with cassis.

Everything about Listen to the Night was elegant. Marble-floored foyer. Plush, royal-blue velvet-covered booths and draperies. Wall sconces dripping with crystal and real candles. Bartenders and bouncers alike sporting tuxedos.

The club had an old-fashioned feel, and Nicky could see why it appealed to her mother. "Great place," she said. "I hope the music lives up to the atmosphere."

"It does," came a deep voice to her left. "You got my personal guarantee."

"Oren!" Cecilia trilled.

A silver-haired man whose tux was perfectly tailored to his stocky body stared down at Nicky.

"Ah, so this is your Nicole," he said, a charming smile softening his craggy features. "Your mama didn't tell me you were such a looker." He took her hand, but rather than shaking it, brushed his lips over her knuckles. "My great pleasure...though I still can't hardly believe my Ceci is old enough to have a grown kid."

Oh, yeah, she could feature her mother with this guy, even though his smooth looks and dashing manner were a little at odds with jargon that indicated a different kind of background.

"I'm pleased to meet you, Mr. Maticek."

"Oren." He slid in next to her mother and wrapped

a possessive arm around her shoulders. "I want you should feel at home here. I got a pretty good chef in the kitchen. Whatever you have a taste for, you order. On the house, of course. Anything for my Ceci's little girl."

"Thank you, but I had dinner hours ago."

"Eat again," he urged. "You don't finish...so what? I recommend the lobster."

"Oren is so very generous," her mother murmured.

She made cow-eyes at the man, and Nicky swallowed hard so the bubble of laughter that threatened to escape her would stay at the back of her throat. Luckily, the singer and her pianist were just taking center stage, so distracting herself from showing her amusement was simple.

Within minutes, they were concentrating on the music. And on the food Oren insisted on ordering. The chef was better than "pretty good," and Nicky was wondering how many miles it would take to run off the calories she consumed.

Despite having a good time, she couldn't help wondering how things were going at the sleep disorder center. Whether or not Flint was exhibiting the traits Dr. Galloway and her technician Dana King were looking for.

The music faded into the background as thoughts of Flint filled her head.

Specifically, what had happened at the warehouse. *And what had almost happened...*

He'd wanted to kiss her again. She'd felt it. Had hungered for it. The hint of danger had sparked Flint's protective instincts, but she didn't know if they were really for her or for the wife and child he hadn't been able to save. She suspected he didn't know for certain, either, and until he did, perhaps his restraint was the best for them both.

Afterward, on her prompting, he'd claimed his being so spooked was an aberration, and he'd refused to discuss the incident further. But Nicky had been shaken to her core by his overreaction. If she'd been frightened, she could only imagine how he'd felt. She was also convinced his constant internalizing did him no good whatsoever and suspected it added to his sleep burden.

If only he could bring himself to work with a professional to resolve the trauma and the guilt...then maybe...just maybe...they would have a chance....

But at what?

Could she ever hold her own against her sister's ghost?

Engrossed in her thoughts, Nicky suddenly realized the music had stopped. The singer and pianist were just leaving the stage. And Oren Maticek was studying her openly.

With a troubled expression, he asked, "So, the joint's okay or not?"

His question made her realize she was frowning, undoubtedly giving him the impression of dissatisfaction. She forced herself to lighten up. To smile.

"More than okay, Oren," she said with sincerity. "I was lost someplace for a moment, that's all. Everything is wonderful. The entertainment. The food. The ambience." She could easily imagine spending a romantic evening there with Flint. "Did you design the club yourself?"

"Nah. I got people with good taste to do that for me. Tell you the truth, this place is my hobby. Actually, I bought it so I could have a place to unwind."

Which must mean he had another business. "From what?"

"Nicole, dear," her mother said pleasantly, "Oren prefers leaving his other interests at the front door."

"Your mama knows what a man needs that goes beyond the basics," Oren said, giving the woman's shoulders a hard squeeze that made her flinch slightly. "Not many of her kind left in this world, I tell you. Uh, as I'm sure you're a more modern woman with different views...no offense."

"None taken," Nicky assured him, flattered that he cared about her feelings.

That he was old-fashioned didn't bother her and probably pleased her mother, who often mourned the old order, which she believed had gotten lost somewhere between feminism and the rocky economy of the past decade and a half. She had always maintained that women were meant to be taken care of, and should only work at something they were passionate about. She certainly wouldn't have passed up a successful career singing if she'd had the choice.

Thinking music must have brought the couple together, Nicky asked, "Did Mom tell you she used to sing in clubs like this before she met my father?"

"That she did. And, you ask me, she's still got a great set of pipes."

"Flatterer," Cecilia said in a flirty voice. She moved closer and slid a hand up his arm.

Which was when Nicky noticed the pearl bracelet encasing her wrist. New. And it looked to be real, which would suit her mother's taste if not her budget. Undoubtedly a present from Oren.

The reason her mother had indicated things were working out better than expected?

"Nah, I mean it, Ceci," he was saying. "You got what it takes to deliver a tune."

Cecilia preened at the compliment, yet somehow managed to maintain a facade of modesty. "In the shower, perhaps. But I'm no longer good enough to sing for my supper."

"Oh, I don't know…"

"Besides, I'm a little too mature."

Now *that* was too much to be believable, Nicky thought. Cecilia Keating was rabid about minimizing her age, making herself out to be as young as she could. Suspicious, she wondered what her mother was up to.

"Too mature for the supper crowd?" Oren was saying. "I mean, we're not talking rock club here."

Her mother went all wide-eyed. "You really think I could?"

"I don't see why not."

"Oren," she said breathlessly, "is this theoretical? Or do you really want me to sing in your club?"

He paused only a heartbeat before saying, "Of course I do. I'm all for it. Anything it takes to make my Ceci happy."

And Nicky sat stunned as the two began talking about Cecilia *Lawrence*'s big comeback. Her mother insisted she had to use her maiden name since that was what her old "fans" would know her by. She was manipulating Oren like a pro.

As she used to do with Alana.

Nicky's glow of enjoyment over the evening faded slightly.

"Listen to us go on when we have a guest," Oren said, turning to Nicky. "We can talk dates and details later. So, do you sing, too?"

"Sorry. Not me. Except for the shower."

"Nicole never could carry a tune."

As she had so many times in the past, her mother made it sound like something she could control. Nicky unclenched her jaw and said, "Not like my sister could."

"Listen, your mama told me about how Alana died. Such a tragedy." He reached over and placed his hand on hers. "You got my condolences."

"Thank you. This past year has been tough."

Smile fading, Cecilia agreed. "A terrible year."

"A parent shouldn't outlive her kid." Oren clucked. "Such heartbreak."

"Especially since my baby would still be alive if *that man* hadn't dragged her off to California…ripping her from the bosom of her loved ones."

Negative energy suddenly seemed to vibrate from her mother. Though she knew she should find a way to neutralize the situation, Nicky couldn't stop herself from defending Flint.

"Alana *was* with her loved ones."

"Her daughter, yes."

"And her husband."

"Who never really cared about her."

"Because he never *proved* it to your satisfaction?" Nicky asked, even as she told *herself* to cool down.

"He couldn't even be faithful to her, taking up with that Jensen woman!"

"You can't cheat on a dead woman. Alana was gone for nearly a year before Flint started seeing Beverly."

Though Nicky almost felt that she and Flint would be doing just that if they gave way to their emotional and physical attraction. At least she would feel that way until he dealt with his grief.

"Who said Alana was dead when that man started his straying? You ought to keep that in mind before you get too involved with him, Nicole."

Oren finally interrupted. "Hey, hey, take it easy, Ceci."

Nicky stared at her mother. All her life she'd lived in Alana's shadow. All her life she'd heard her mother making Alana's decisions without contest. Until Flint had come along, that is. Did she really hate her son-in-law so much that she would make up lies about him?

She feared Flint wasn't the only one who needed grief counseling. In reality, many times over the years she'd thought her mother could use professional help when she'd been *too* focused on Alana. Not that she'd ever suggested as much.

And lately, she'd thought her mother had seemed more balanced. At least most of the time.

Maybe she'd been manipulating her, as well.

"We've been having a real nice night here," Oren was saying. "Let's concentrate on enjoying good company and good music...uh, as soon as break time is over."

Checking his watch with the air of a man who took charge of any situation, he looked around as if willing the performers to return to the stage.

Cecilia sniffed and settled against the booth back. "Yes, of course, Oren." She sounded, if she didn't exactly look, contrite. "What was I thinking?"

Nicky smiled as if she, too, agreed, when as far as she was concerned, the night had already ended on a sour note.

Chapter Eleven

The next morning didn't begin any better for her.

Awake half the night because she'd been troubled over the way her mother had manipulated Oren, Nicky overslept. Now she had no time for so much as a cup of coffee if she was to arrive at Lakeshore Medical Center before Flint was ready to leave.

But she had to make time for the dog.

Nothing like a predawn walk in subzero weather to wake a sleepyhead. Yawning, she gingerly danced over the slippery pavement behind him.

"C'mon, Scraps, I have to get on the road."

But urging the dog to hurry didn't make him find his spot any faster. And it was while Nicky impatiently waited that she had her first inkling of something being wrong. The notion began vaguely, but quickly jelled.

Her car...where was it?

Though she gazed hard through the dark, she couldn't spot its familiar contours.

Not having a regular space, she had to take her chances on street parking like most other city apartment dwellers. Each new day brought a new location. Because she taught, she was pretty lucky. She usually arrived home from work early enough for a choice of spots. Late at night was another story. Still, she rarely had a hike to get home. Normally she could at least see the car from her building's front door.

Not so this morning.

Stomach plummeting, Nicky convinced herself the streetlights must be playing tricks on her. Scraps tugged at the leash and she followed like an automaton, while aiming her gaze up and down the street.

No Escort.

"Hey, boy, let's go this way," she said, panic changing her direction.

She dragged the dog until he got the idea she was serious and took the lead again. But this trek was no more successful than the first.

So Nicky ducked around a corner and raced halfway down the street before stopping cold.

"Wait a minute. This is ridiculous. I *know* where I parked!"

Concentrating, she visualized herself at half-past midnight...driving west up the street that fronted her building...parking in a spot so small it would have quelled the faint of heart...walking back to the apartment house.

Though admittedly upset and a little distracted, Nicky was absolutely certain that she'd parked halfway down the block from her front entrance.

But even as she raced back the way they'd come to take another look, Nicky accepted the truth....

"WE'RE ONTO SOMETHING." Looking over the recorded results of Flint's second night in the center, Dr. Galloway sounded satisfied. "What we have here is a classic pattern of a sleepwalker. Rather than the normal smooth ascent from deep sleep through light sleep

into REM sleep, you show an unnaturally long beginning deep sleep cycle interrupted by abrupt arousals.
Look here.''

She indicated a few areas of scratches, which looked
like so much gibberish to Flint.

"I can't say I remember being out of bed at all."

"That's because you weren't. But, given another
night or two here, you might. At any rate, last night,
when Dana spoke to you via the intercom, you settled
back down."

"Which I don't remember."

"Again, that's not unusual during non-REM. But I
was wondering…" Removing her half-moon glasses,
the psychotherapist set them down on the lab table
where she'd spread out the records Dana had turned
over before leaving. "Do you recall dreaming?"

Flint did, indeed. "I spent the night searching
through buildings and rubble for something I couldn't
find. No matter where I looked, it was always just out
of reach."

He hadn't been able to find Alana and Megan until
it was too late, he thought. Were they what he'd been
searching for in the dream, then?

Or had he been trying to get to Nicky?

"So does that knock me out from having this disorder?" Flint was surprised at the sudden disappointment that filled him at the possibility. When had having Dr. Galloway's backing become so important to
him? "You said I wasn't supposed to remember anything."

"Not about what you might have been dreaming—or more probably were thinking about—in non-
REM sleep," she clarified. "That's when you would
be left with those powerful images and sounds you

say you've been experiencing during the sleepwalking incidents. But you made up for a bit of that REM time you lost the night before.'' Again, she indicated areas on his charts. ''And that's when you had the dreams about searching for something you'd lost.''

''Which I told Dana about,'' he said, vaguely recalling the technician prompting him with questions several times.

''I was there to observe, as well,'' Dr. Galloway said. ''Did anything unusual happen yesterday? Or were you worrying about something in particular before falling asleep? Other than the upcoming trial.''

''You could say that.''

Flint told the psychotherapist in detail about the incident at the warehouse and his physical reaction to what he'd imagined had been happening.

His thinking about how he'd scared Nicky made him wonder what was keeping her. Hopefully, a good time the night before—maybe she was still sleeping.

Trying not to worry about her, too, he said, ''I guess I went a little overboard imagining the structure was really going to collapse around our ears.''

''It sounds as though you were experiencing a flashback, Mr. Armstrong. For a moment, you relived something having to do with the earthquake.''

''Exactly.''

''Has this ever happened to you before?''

''I can't say that it has. Terrific. Something new.'' Which didn't bode well for his future. Every time he turned around, his situation seemed to worsen. ''Maybe I'm going nuts and should be locked away.''

''Or maybe you're at the point where you need to resolve what happened to you by exploring your feelings rather than continuing to pretend they don't exist,'' she said in a kindly manner.

Basically what Nicky had been harping on for nearly a year now.

"You think something as simple as talking would do the trick?"

"There's nothing simple about sleep disorders, Mr. Armstrong, though we can usually classify a patient a little more easily than we can you."

"Classify?"

"Well, the person could be a natural disaster survivor...or could have a case of post-traumatic stress syndrome. Or he could have lost a loved one... possibly a parent who lost a child, which is far more damaging. He could feel responsible for not preventing some tragedy...feel guilty for being alive. We rarely have a patient who seems to embody all of the above."

Flint felt as if she'd delivered him a double-whammy. "Then I *am* a major head case."

"Working out your feelings with someone who is trained to help would be in your best interests," Dr. Galloway said. "So would joining a support group— people in similar if less serious circumstances. And here at the sleep disorder center, we can teach you how to deal with the dreams you remember. If you're open to it, you can know when you're dreaming and control the situation. As for future non-REM incidents, we can give you some tips to keep yourself and others safe. Hopefully, as you gain insight...and lose some of that guilt...you'll stop sleepwalking altogether."

He asked, "You think that's really possible?"

"I'm certainly hopeful."

"No promises, though."

"Promises?" Expression rueful, Dr. Galloway shook her head. "I'm afraid not. But an educated guess? If it were me, Mr. Armstrong, *I'd* go for it!"

Something to consider seriously, Flint decided. Had he taken Nicky's advice in the first place, perhaps the sleepwalking incidents would never have begun.

And maybe Beverly would still be alive.

NICKY HOTFOOTED it down the corridor just as Flint left the sleep disorder center. Fists jammed into his jacket pockets, he appeared anything but happy, but his frown lightened when he saw her.

"There you are. I was starting to worry about you," he admitted as they met in the middle of the hallway. "I guess you overslept."

"That and I had to take public transportation."

"Your car wouldn't start? Why didn't you just call and tell me rather than coming all the way down here?"

Puffing because of her run from the bus stop, she gasped, "It's gone—vanished right off the street."

"Stolen? You're sure?"

"I looked everywhere."

His frown reasserting itself, Flint asked, "Did you make out a police report?"

"Not yet. I just called it in."

"That's the first order of business, then. We can take a taxi to the nearest district office."

Realizing how unpleasant that would be for Flint—considering his circumstances with the law—she said, "Listen, I don't need my hand held or anything."

"I think you do, and if anyone is going to hold it, I'll do the honors."

Flint's enveloping her hand in his made Nicky feel all too vulnerable, something she hadn't wanted to admit even to herself. He studied her closely, then without words, pulled her into his arms. A perfect fit. Her heart thudded, not only from the close contact.

He was reaching out to give *her* succor for a change, she realized. Another positive step. He was rediscovering his humanity more rapidly than she thought possible.

Nicky was happy for that, of course, despite part of her worrying that, once he had his life back, he would no longer need her.

"Are *you* all right?" Flint murmured into her hair.

"Other than feeling violated?" Curbing the urge to cling to him and have a good cry, she shrugged and pushed herself back, showing him a brave face. "I'll survive."

Physically, anyway.

Nicky wasn't about to bring up the financial blow the theft had dealt her. All her liquid assets were tied up in Flint's bond. Although there was a slight chance of recovery, the police had as much as told her not to hold her breath. Given a large deductible, added to the fact that getting replacement value was doubtful, Nicky feared she wouldn't be able to buy another car nearly as nice.

Before Flint could probe and get all that out of her, she asked, "So what happened with you?"

"Dr. Galloway is convinced we're on the right track. She hopes another few nights in the center will prove it."

"Well, that's good news."

At least something was going right.

She kept that fact in mind later in the day when she

called her insurance company from the ACT offices. Making her claim proved to be more painful than dealing with the police had been. The interrogator at the other end seemed to be less believing of her when she swore she'd locked the car up tight before leaving it for the night. The police had been more philosophical, treating her case as business as usual. Nothing odd about a decent car disappearing off the streets of Chicago.

In the meantime, Flint was finessing the computer for the social security numbers of Eric Jensen and Sid Shelton. By the time she got off the phone, he not only had the identifiers, but had run credit checks on both men, as well.

"For all his money troubles, Shelton comes off smelling as sweet as a rose. Jensen's records are spotty, though. A lot of credit card shuffling. Looks like he was taking money from Peter to pay Paul."

"So what does that mean?"

"That we should let Phelps dig deeper. He should be able to make quick work of finding out about any investments shared with Beverly...or any life insurance policies...just in case. I thought I would call his office while you tracked down those license plate numbers. I already brought up the database."

She parked herself before the computer and groaned. "Only nine hundred and ninety-nine possible alphanumeric combinations. What are *you* going to do with the rest of *your* day?"

"It won't take you all day," he assured her. "Not if you stipulate the make and model of the vehicle. Let the computer do your work for you."

Once satisfied she was into the loop, he let her take over while he contacted the lawyer's office.

Grateful to have something other than her missing car occupy her thoughts, Nicky was thrilled when the actual number of license plates was reduced to less than three dozen. And by looking over those and eliminating possibles by age of the vehicle or address of the owner—she didn't think someone from downstate Illinois or the far-reaching suburbs was following her around—she further reduced the number to seven.

"Now that's workable."

Though scanning the information on the candidates didn't switch on any lightbulbs. She didn't have a clue as to which of the five men or two women could be following her. Hopefully, Flint would fare better.

Nicky printed the records, wondering how to connect any of the seven to Sid Shelton.

Shelton...a known chop shop operator...a man who dealt in stolen car parts...who arranged for cars to be stolen...

Hers?

Stunned by the idea, Nicky wondered if it was possible. Had Shelton chosen to put her out of commission by taking her car? Or was he paying her back because she wouldn't keep her nose out of his business?

Eager to share her speculation with Flint, she didn't get the opportunity. Even as he hung up the phone, Terrence walked into the room, every fiber of his thin body appearing wired.

"My man. I bear news."

"About Hector Villada?"

Terrence nodded. "You can cross that homie off your list."

"How so?" Nicky asked.

"He couldn't have done the Jensen woman...not when he and his lady were already dead."

Nicky started. "Who says? Villada's sister seemed to think he was alive." And that had been a mere two days before.

"His family thought he was alive because he had a way of disappearing for unspecified amounts of time."

"But on Christmas?"

Terrence shrugged. "Maybe they thought he was in trouble again and lying low. And no one had forced their way into his lady's apartment yet. A neighbor got upset by the smell and finally called the cops yesterday. From what they could tell, Villada killed Isabelle Rodriguez—beat her to death—then shot himself in the head."

Nicky's stomach turned at the image that conjured. "Not what you would call quiet deaths. And no one called the police?"

"Most people don't get involved in someone else's domestic squabbles."

The news brought a pall over them all. An abuser finally killing his victim, Nicky thought, sick at heart.

Like Beverly?

Flint must have been on the same wavelength, because he said, "Let's make it a point to check on Jensen's alibi."

They decided on a visit to River West Realty. The plan was easy and one Nicky could execute alone. No need to alert anyone else with Flint's presence. He decided to wait for her at a bookstore down the street.

The large real estate company involved in renovating as well as selling space in old industrial buildings near the Chicago River was located in one of its pet projects. Her insides fluttering with nerves, Nicky entered the spacious offices overlooking the North Branch. The receptionist, an older woman in a designer suit, immediately put her at ease with a friendly smile.

"Can I help you?"

"I hope so. Eric Jensen sent me."

"Mr. Jensen?" The receptionist reached for the telephone. "I didn't know he was expecting his paperwork—"

"No! Uh, I mean this isn't business. It's about the party on Christmas Eve." Nicky tried to sound natural—she'd never been good at lying. "Eric had this really nice muffler, but now he can't find it. He thought maybe he left it behind."

"Oh, no. I made sure he was wearing it."

Nicky started. "You did?" Though she'd figured a muffler was a common enough object, how would she have guessed the receptionist would have noticed it?

"He was coming down with some nasty bug...the reason he left the party so early."

When "How early?" slipped out of her mouth, Nicky wanted to kick herself.

Why couldn't she learn to think before she spoke?

Though the receptionist did give her an odd look, she didn't seem suspicious. "He left well before midnight, when Santa passed out everyone's presents. The messenger service did deliver Mr. Jensen's?"

"Of course," Nicky bluffed, praying she wouldn't be asked for details. "So, he had his muffler."

"Though he didn't have the good sense to wear it until I pointed out that cold air on an exposed throat wouldn't make him feel better." The receptionist clucked and shook her head. "Not a big surprise, though, knowing men and all."

"Men," Nicky echoed, knowing full well that Eric Jensen hadn't been too sick to attend his ex-wife's wake.

Thanking the receptionist, she headed straight for the bookstore. Finding Flint browsing the magazine rack, she hauled him onto the street where she repeated the conversation almost verbatim.

"So Jensen didn't have an alibi for the night Beverly died, after all," he mused.

"Do you think Shelton can come up with one that sticks any better?"

"We'd have to ask him."

Ignoring his sarcasm, she said, "Then let's do it."

"You're not serious."

"And while we're at it...let's ask him about my car."

"Your..." Flint's eyes glinted strangely as he cursed. "I didn't even think of Shelton."

"Start thinking about a way to get my car back if he's got his greasy hands on it."

"Nicky, be realistic. It may already be too late."

Undoubtedly, he was correct. Even so, Flint agreed a visit was worth a shot, which meant a trip home to pick up his junker of a Pontiac.

"This thing's a boat," she groused as they sailed toward the first of several addresses they'd picked up from Terrence's files.

"Probably why no one's ever tried to steal it."

He had a point.

The first address proved to be dated. An Everything for a Buck emporium had replaced Shelton's old business. The second had been burned out long before. Luckily, they hit pay dirt on the third. The man himself was in and agreed to see them.

Ensconced in a luxurious office that countered the ratty car parts store that fronted it, he watched them approach through narrowed gaze. "Well, well, if it ain't the future jailbird come to pay his respects."

"Who said anything about respect?" Flint asked.

"This is my turf. You're welcome to go back out the way you came."

"Then you wouldn't know why we're here."

Shelton looked from Flint to her. The way he said "Car trouble?" made Nicky gnash her teeth. Following Flint's orders, however, she was letting him do the talking.

"You could say that," Flint agreed. "We're looking for an Escort. Last year's model. Red with a gray interior."

"What do I look like? A broker?"

Unable to stop herself, Nicky suggested, "How about a car thief?"

"You got a mouth on you."

"So I've been told." *And now that she'd opened it...* "What about it, Shelton? What have you done with my car?"

Expression as innocent as a babe, he protested, "Someone has misguided you."

"I don't think so."

Flint surreptitiously squeezed her arm to stop her from pursuing the argument. "We can settle this among ourselves...or not."

A short silence was followed by Shelton's "That a threat, Armstrong?"

"Take it how you will. But if Nicky's car should happen to turn up in the next twenty-four hours...no more said."

"And if not?"

"There are always consequences."

The men glared at each other, reminding Nicky of two rutting bucks sizing each other up over territory.

Then Shelton broke the connection, saying, "Consequences goes two ways. Remember that." He waved a disinterested hand. "Let yourself out."

When Flint ushered her toward the door, Nicky thought he'd forgotten about their original purpose until he stopped at the threshold and turned back toward his nemesis.

"By the way, Shelton, I hope you had a fruitful Christmas."

"Ain't my holiday...but I can get into the *spirits* anyhow." He barked a laugh and showed off his capped teeth. "I take it this is leading up to somethin'. Don't play cute, Armstrong. Spit it out. What's on your mind?"

"I was merely wondering how you spent your Christmas Eve."

Shelton didn't hesitate. "Working in St. Anthony's soup kitchen, which happened to stay open all night. Ask Father Cassivitis or Alderman Johnnie Monroe if you need corroboration. Their gig."

"I may do just that."

Feeling Shelton's dark gaze bore into her back as they left, Nicky waited until they were inside the Pontiac before asking, "Do you think it washes?"

"The alibi? I don't doubt Shelton has it locked up tight as a drum. We'll check it out, though, to be sure."

"What about my car?"

Flint shook his head. "I hope you gave it a fond farewell."

"YOU LOOK LIKE you have lots on your mind tonight," Dana King told Flint as she secured the last of the electrodes.

"Too much. I'll be surprised if I get *any* sleep."

"Uh-huh." Laughing, she said, "Now don't let the bedbugs bite."

After which she left Flint to face the long night ahead.

Conflicted anew about his circumstances, he'd reported to the sleep disorder center alone. He'd had to insist before Nicky had given way. Thankfully. At least he knew she would be safe for the night.

Even so, how was he going to sleep knowing that Eric Jensen had lied about his alibi?

That Sid Shelton might have been responsible for the theft of Nicky's car?

That Phelps had cleared the way so he could move back into his own home the very next day?

While moving back into the house would be difficult, Flint knew he needed to be there. He needed to face his rocky marriage with Alana. Needed to face Beverly's death.

To remember Megan.

Perhaps that was his biggest sin of all—allowing grief and despair and guilt to wipe away his memories of his only child.

But Nicky's faith and prodding had whipped him out of his self-imposed cocoon, and he could no longer hide from himself. Apathy might be safe. But it wasn't healthy. And it wasn't for him. Assuming he didn't end up at the wrong end of a lethal injection, he was going to live fully again.

And if he was very, very lucky, Nicky would stick around until he could.

The simple truth was that he felt more for the woman he'd once thought of as a kid sister than gratitude or affection or simple lust. He loved her...was *in love with* her...and suspected she might be in the same predicament.

Not that they could act on their feelings. Not now. Not until the demons that drove him to unknowing violence were put to rest.

He couldn't act on his need for Nicky lest he hurt her in some way.

She couldn't be his next victim...not even by accident.

THE EARTH WAS shifting...rumbling...screaming.

Earthquake...

"Alana! Megan!"

He had to get to them.

The floor shifted. Walls collapsed. Earth stilled. Not so his heart.

His foot nicked something soft.

A body...Alana...open eyes staring...

And a greater fear filled him.

What had once been the door to his daughter's bedroom hung twisted on its hinges, the black, endless opening beyond luring him...

"Daddy?"

A faint cry...real or imagined?

He forced himself inside, detected the shadow of Megan's bed amidst the debris.

Another whisper, "Daddy?" drowned by an inhuman scream.

What was left of the floor shifted, her corner of the room swallowed whole. Wild with panic, bare-handed, he attacked the ever-shifting rubble.

"Megan, honey, Daddy's here! Don't be afraid! I'll get you out, I promise!"

He dug and dug, but for every fragment he removed, two more took its place. He worked like a madman until his hands were raw and his mind was numb....

Until rescuers dragged him, kicking and screaming, to safety...

"MR. ARMSTRONG... Flint?" came a distant voice even as his daughter's terrified plea echoed over and over in his head. "You're all right now. You're safe...."

The voice clarified into one he recognized. Heart pounding wildly, Flint concentrated.

Focused.

Awakened.

Breath ragged, free of the electrodes, not remembering a thing that he'd done, he stood in the middle of the sleep room and stared at the destruction around him.

Ripped sheets piled in one corner...shredded mattress lying cockeyed against a wall...bed frame bent and teetering on its side.

He'd done this. As always, he was horrified.

The door opened. Dana King wasn't laughing now. Neither was Dr. Galloway, who accompanied her. Her expression was both grave and sympathetic.

Flint knew then that she would testify in his behalf.

Chapter Twelve

Knowing for certain that Dr. Galloway would testify for Flint, if the case against him did make it to trial, gave Nicky a modicum of comfort, although proving that someone else was guilty of murder would have made her feel even better. At odd moments, when she least expected it, the image of Flint flinging Beverly against the dining room table troubled her.

Being that it was New Year's Eve, however, they were at a forced halt in their private investigation. Not to mention at an impasse. She really didn't know what else they could do other than identify the owner of the vehicle that had been conspicuous by its absence since their visit to the deserted warehouse.

"We should have asked Shelton about the Buick," Nicky said as they scoured the meat section of his local grocery store for the perfect steaks.

"Like he'd volunteer the truth. How about these?" Flint asked, holding up two filets.

"My mouth is already watering."

He threw the meat in the cart, already nearly full. The problem with shopping on an empty stomach was that everything looked too good to pass up.

They headed for home through a snowy dusk. The

temperature had already dropped and the weather fore-
casters predicted four to six inches and a severe drop
in temperature. Nicky snuggled against Scraps, who
shared the front seat with them and would spend the
evening at Flint's.

His own home now available to him, Flint had volunteered to make them dinner, and Nicky was looking
forward to spending a quiet evening in his company.
An evening that might have romantic overtones if they
weren't going to be in the same house he'd shared
with her sister.

Not wanting to think about Alana, she instead focused on the Buick. The printout of vehicles and owners hadn't rung any bells for Flint, either. If only
they'd gotten a better look at the license plate. Something kept nagging her about it. She stared into the
swirling snow and visualized. The first image that
came to her was that of a bird.

"It was a vanity license plate!" she said. "Why it
didn't occur to me before..."

"Do you remember if there was anyone on the list
with the initials LTM?"

"No, but...what if we were wrong about the M? I
wasn't sure about it. Remember? It could have been
an N."

"So we'll run another check."

Always one for instant gratification, Nicky couldn't
help griping. "Too bad we have to wait."

"Is first thing tomorrow morning soon enough for
you?"

She started. "New Year's Day? You're kidding.
Are your former partners so driven they work on holidays?"

"Try trusting. I have a key." He appeared resigned. "So how soon do you want to leave for downtown?"

And give up their evening? "Tomorrow morning sounds just fine."

Only a few blocks from her apartment, his house sat on an oddly shaped lot directly on the bank of the Chicago River's North Branch. While surrounding owners had terraced or otherwise cultivated the long, steep drop to the river below, Flint had chosen to leave his slope natural with trees and bushes, wild grasses and flowers. The area was a paradise in the milder months. But now the bank was frozen over to the water's edge, holding a stark, cold beauty.

The house itself was a typical Chicago bungalow—a single story of original living space with a pitched roof over an attic that had long ago been converted to a master bedroom and nursery. Rooms that Flint studiously avoided. Since the earthquake, he'd been sleeping in the guest bedroom. Understandably, he'd now ruled that room out, as well. Luckily his home office was furnished with a futon.

If much else untoward happened, Nicky thought, he'd be sleeping in the detached garage.

Flint pulled the car off the alley onto his property directly behind the rear door. As they grabbed bags of groceries from the trunk, Scraps ran circles through the heavy, wet snow, which was already icing up.

"Careful," Flint warned when she slid along the sidewalk.

"I should have brought my ice skates."

He unlocked the back door for her. "Then you could have provided the evening's entertainment."

His teasing expression made her pulse thrum. He

was acting like his old self...the Flint she'd fallen for the first time she'd seen him.

"You mean I have to entertain you?"

"Haven't you ever heard of singing for your supper?"

Reminded of her mother's cruel comment about her not being able to carry a tune, she grimaced. Since she didn't want the evening to start on a negative note, she pushed all such thoughts to the back of her mind and hurried inside.

"Give me your jacket and I'll hang it up," Flint volunteered as Nicky set her bags on the kitchen table.

She stripped off her outer garments and handed them to him. "Wow, it's nice and warm in here."

"Or really cold outside." He headed for the coat closet in the other room.

"I'm glad we're not going out tonight," she said, opening the refrigerator door for a look. "The forecast is twenty-five below with the wind chill factor."

"That wet snow'll turn to ice fast," he agreed. "The last thing we need is a car accident."

"Especially since *my* car is gone. Then we'd really be out of commission." Nicky picked up an orange that had shriveled and molded in spots. "Yuk. When was the last time you cleaned out your refrigerator?"

Returning to the kitchen, Flint said, "I'm going to plead the Fifth on that one."

"You could use a fifth...of alcohol," she joked, tossing the orange into the garbage. "To help kill off the slime in here."

They disposed of several other questionable items and quickly cleaned the appliance before unpacking the groceries. When the phone rang, they were only half through.

Flint fetched the wireless from its cradle on the wall. "Armstrong here." He paused, then said, "Phelps," as if for her benefit. "Hold on." He covered the mouthpiece. "Would you mind putting the rest away?"

She shrugged. "Go."

Leaving the room, he gave the lawyer the lowdown on his experience at the sleep center the night before.

Scraps started to follow, then changed his mind, going to the back door, where he stood whistling through his nose instead. Nicky figured some small animal must be cutting across Flint's property.

"Good boy," she said, patting his side and momentarily distracting him.

She went back to her groceries and he to his watch. The whistle grew into more anxious sounds. Nicky glanced at him. He was on the alert, his body tense, his concentration focused.

"What's up, boy?"

She glanced through the window to see what was out there, but the dark and still-falling snow made it impossible. Could be kids cutting across the property below the ridge. Or a rat looking for food—the downside of living on the river. She shivered at the thought of coming face-to-nose with a rodent and went back to restocking the refrigerator. And while Scraps continued to be restless, his anxiety gradually abated, and he trotted out of the room, ostensibly in search of Flint.

The last item in place, Nicky realized she hadn't seen the butter. Either the package hadn't made it into a bag at the store, or it had fallen out in the car.

Grabbing his keys from where Flint had thrown them on the table, she braved the dark and gritted her teeth against the cold. Maybe she should have gone in search of her jacket first. Thankfully, the errand would only take a minute. The ground was even more slippery than it had been when they'd gone in, so she carefully picked her way to the rear of the car.

The key pierced a thin layer of ice sealing the trunk lock, and Nicky figured things were only going to get worse. She lifted the lid—and there it was. Grabbing the butter, she decided to repark the car to protect it from the elements.

The garage perched on the riverbank, and Nicky knew it took a bit of strategy to get such a large vehicle inside. She'd seen Flint do it enough times.

The Pontiac really *was* a boat, she thought, climbing behind the wheel. Having to make a partial U-turn at the edge of an incline on icy ground was not too thrilling.

Nicky tensed as she put the car in drive. Taking it slow and easy, she maneuvered around the natural bend in the land and was lining herself up with the garage opening when a sharp noise startled her into kicking the accelerator.

The car jerked, and before Nicky could think, spun and slid toward the bank.

Heart pounding, she kept her head, taking her foot off the accelerator while steering into the direction of the slide. When she gently tapped the brake, the car jerked again and whipped even more sharply to the side. Trying not to panic, she did her best to regain control. But not only had there had been no room for error, the vehicle seemed to have a mind of its own....

Sliding...sliding...sliding...

A scream caught in her throat as the precipice

rushed toward her. For a moment, time stood still and her life flashed before her eyes, Flint's image sticking.

Her stomach fell with the car as it slid downhill sideways.

She thought to get out before the vehicle hit the water, but she couldn't move fast enough. Her fingers barely curled around the door handle, when the car smashed to a teetering, teeth-jarring stop. Nicky flew across the seat, whacking her right shoulder in the process. Then, because the car was off-kilter, driver's side tilted downhill, she slid back and piled up against the door.

Shaky if basically unhurt, she found the handle and popped open the door, then literally fell out of the car onto the icy surface. The impact tobogganed her downward several more yards. Landing mere feet from the water's edge, she lay facedown for a moment, trying to catch her breath. In the distance, a dog barked furiously.

"Scraps?" she called weakly.

Icy cold seeped through her clothing. Carefully, she pushed herself to her feet. A tentative step up lost her several inches. She tried again and lost even more ground, slipping too close to the river for comfort. And above her, the car clung precariously to the tree that had stopped its free fall.

Nicky focused. She had to get out of its path. Just in case...

She crabbed sideways, searching for an easier path back up the hill even as she heard the dog straight overhead. His whistles were punctuated by a sharp bark.

Barely able to see him, she said, "Scraps, where's Flint? Go find Flint!"

Even as the dog lunged back toward the house, she heard Flint call, "Hey, Nicky, what's going on?"

"Thank God." She yelled, "Down here!"

The momentary distraction causing a misstep.

Her foot went right out from under her and she shot over the embankment. Though her stomach did a wheelie, the plunge into the icy river proved anything but thrilling.

"Nicky? What happened? Are you all right?"

"I would be, if I were a polar bear," she gasped, somehow finding her feet.

She could see Flint against the snow-covered bank. He was searching for a way down to her. While the water was only up to her waist, she couldn't get a grip on anything that would take her onto solid land.

"Careful, or you'll be in the same boat!" she warned.

Boat. The Pontiac. What had started as a giggle had ended as a pathetic hiccup. She imagined herself trapped in the car as it sank in the middle of the river. If that tree hadn't halted its descent...

Only by the grace of God had she been spared a horrible end.

"I'll get you out of there, I promise, but I need to find something I can use to haul you out first." He tore away, yelling, "Hang on!"

Not about to stand still in the meantime, Nicky inched through the water, continuing to search for a way out. Some crevice where she could wedge a hand or foot.

Nothing.

She started to shiver. Her feet were lumping into blocks of ice, and her legs were beginning to burn with the cold. And her bare fingers—she could hardly move them.

How long did frostbite take?

To warm herself as she tried climbing onto the bank despite the seeming impossibility, she imagined Flint's arms around her. Holding her. Comforting her. She imagined telling him how she felt...imagined him reciprocating.

Her footing gave way and she fell back into the water with a splash.

"Damn!"

She'd never felt so cold. So vulnerable. So maudlin.

What if it was too late? What if she didn't survive? Then she'd never have the chance to find out if Flint felt the same way she did.

More barking signaled his return.

"Scraps, stay," she heard him say. Then, to her— "Nicky, can you move toward me?"

"Not up."

"I mean south. My neighbor's property. That's the easiest path."

"I'll try," she agreed, forcing her way against the current.

Had she been meant to die, she told herself, that tree wouldn't have stopped the car. She needed to stay focused and positive.

"You'll be all right," Flint reassured her, his voice quickly drawing closer. "I promise I'll make you warm and safe in no time."

He kept talking. The words were meaningless, but the seductive sound of his voice lured her ever closer. At the same time, he was making his way downhill, a long and narrow pole in one hand.

"Only a little farther," he said.

The riverbed had risen beneath her feet, so the water was shallower, easier to cut through. The gap between them narrowed until she was almost directly below him. And the rise here seemed to be less steep.

"Can you grab on to this?"

Hanging on to a small tree trunk for support, he extended the pole, which proved to be the handle of a rake.

"I think so." She reached for it, her fingers stopping barely an inch from the tines. A sound of frustration escaped her.

"Try again."

He stretched longer. She reached harder. Finally, her hand met cold metal.

With effort, she threaded her stiff fingers through the tines and, ignoring the pain, gripped the tool as best she could. "Okay. Now what?"

"Take a step up and don't let go."

The first step was a small one—mere inches—but allowed him a better grip on the handle. A second small step and a third added a bit of leverage. He began to pull. Hanging on for dear life, she fought herself free of the river.

Stumbling onto the bank, she would have fallen to her knees if Flint hadn't let go of the tree and swooped forward to hook an arm around her waist.

"Thank God!" he said fervently, pulling her close just as she'd imagined him doing.

Nicky clung to him. He'd become her lifeline even as she'd been his for the past year.

"Thank *you*," she murmured, filled with the urge to say so much more.

He smoothed the wet hair from her face and peered at her intently. "Are you all right?"

Overwhelmed by the wealth of emotion flowing between them, she nodded. "I am now that you're here."

"Nicky, if anything had happened to you..."

Her heart pounded. Was he going to declare his feelings? "What?"

He cursed, then lowered his head, his lips covering hers...softening them...molding them.

His kiss was desperate, as if he needed to convince himself that she was unharmed. Joy filled Nicky, who returned the kiss with pent-up emotions of her own, but the gratification of knowing that he really did care couldn't banish the effects of a subzero night. She couldn't control the tremors of her flesh trying to warm itself.

As if suddenly realizing this, Flint released her. "Let's get you inside." Using the rake as a staff on the slippery incline, he kept an arm firmly around her while sweeping her upward toward a barking Scraps. "You'll be a lot warmer in a few minutes."

A promise that Nicky took to heart.

ONCE ON FLAT GROUND, Flint dropped the rake and lifted Nicky, meaning to carry her the rest of the way. She wrapped her arms around his neck and murmured his name. The seductive whisper got to him. The fact that he'd almost lost her really hit home as he rushed her toward the house. His chest tightened painfully. Thank God, the dog had sensed something wrong, and they'd come to her rescue in time.

"Almost there," he murmured.

Nicky was shivering against his chest and no wonder. Her wet clothes were icing up. She could be subject to hypothermia if he didn't get her warm fast. And he didn't rule out frostbite.

"Sorry about your c-car."

"Don't worry about it."

"I heard this weird s-sound and it went out of control. I think it's a goner."

He hugged her closer. "You survived, the only thing that counts."

Not like Megan. His daughter had called to him for help, too, but he hadn't gotten to *her* in time.

Scraps reached the rear door first, then whistled through his nose as if telling Flint to hurry.

"Good boy. You deserve a steak of your own tonight."

Once inside, he kicked the door closed behind them and kept on, straight into the bathroom. There he set Nicky on her feet, and only after making certain she could stand on her own, reluctantly let go. Knowing she would be safe now, he allowed himself to cave when he turned away from her and started the shower. The tightness in his chest finally subsided. He took a deep breath while thanking the fates that someone he cared about had been spared for once.

Someone he loved...

He couldn't deny that he did love Nicky. Not that he could tell her so. Not yet...if ever. He had to straighten out his life first. He couldn't ruin hers.

Or possibly end it.

"Get out of those wet clothes fast." The no-nonsense order was meant to cover his surfeit of emotion.

"I'm trying."

What she was doing was getting tangled up in the waterlogged sweater. He freed her. Then, steeling himself against any inappropriate response, he removed her thermal undershirt, as well. Quickly skirting his gaze back to her normally animated face, which was now drawn and pinched from the shock and cold, he wrapped a thick dry towel around her bared torso and gently rubbed some warmth into her shoulders. He fought the urge to take her in his arms and never let go.

"Can you feel everything?"

Her breath catching, she murmured, "Oh, yes."

Her nose was already beginning to glow with renewed warmth, and when he covered her ears with his hands to check for frostbite, he asked, "All the appendages?"

She nodded. "Those, too. I'm tingling—"

"Like they're on fire?" he finished.

"Parts of me are."

Satisfied her ears were all right, Flint carefully checked her hands. While her fingers were white and cold, the flesh was still soft and springy. He lifted his sweater and placed her palms on his stomach, then covered the backs of her hands with his own.

"Feel better?" he asked, ignoring the urgency that immediately sprang to his groin.

Eyes wide, she swallowed hard and bobbed her head. "Much."

Steam from the shower filled the room, curling around them. He sucked in the heavy, humid air as he tried to steady himself. He could feel his own heartbeat, hear the rush of his blood running through his head.

Fighting his baser instincts, he let go of her hands. "Sit, so I can check your feet and toes."

She curled her fingers around the towel and slid

onto the hamper. He removed her boots and socks and warmed her feet as he inspected them.

"Looks okay."

He wasn't, though. Touching her so intimately was proving to be more than he could handle. He straightened and indicated her leggings.

"Uh, you can manage, right?"

Color flushed her cheeks, but he wasn't certain if it was from the warming process or sheer embarrassment.

"I suppose so."

Flint turned his back on her and adjusted the water temperature. "Keep it warm, not hot," he warned her. "I'll get some water going for tea."

"You need to get warm, too," she insisted. "I got you all wet. You'd better take off *your* clothes."

His back still to her, Flint started, then decided he was reading more into the suggestion than she'd meant. He joked, "You can't be too bad off since you're giving orders again."

When he turned around, however, he realized she'd shucked the leggings. Unless he was mistaken, she was wearing nothing at all beneath the towel.

"The minute you get out of the shower, cover your head," he ordered her, making tracks before he lost his. "If you need help, yell."

"Help!"

Flint froze at the door. He didn't dare turn back lest he lose his will to leave her be.

IN THE HOPES that she wasn't asking for rejection, Nicky repeated herself. "I said, 'Help.'"

"*Nicky...*"

"Don't *Nicky* me. You promised you'd make me

warm and safe." Though the shivering had abated, she was still chilled to her bones and, worse, feeling very much out on a limb. "All I'm asking is that you keep your promise."

"You *are* safe...and the water will warm you up."

"But *you'd* do a better job," she insisted, nearly choking on the words. She'd never thrown herself at a man before. Dropping the towel, she said, "I *need* your warmth, Flint," then stepped into the shower without drawing the curtain.

When he still didn't move, she backed against the wall and closed her eyes. *Great.* A shudder that had nothing to do with her being cold shot through her. She'd been so certain... Other than not knowing how she was going to face him, she could deal with her mistake, she guessed.

A little humiliation never killed anyone.

"You're not getting the full benefit of the water back there."

The shower's noise had muffled his approach. Nicky raised her gaze to the sight she most wanted to see—Flint wearing nothing but an intense expression. He stepped inside and pulled the curtain. The space suddenly shrank. Her mouth went dry and her pulse surged as he closed in on her.

"I'm not up on my first aid." She returned her hands to the spot on his stomach where he'd placed them earlier. "Maybe you can show me how it's done."

"You've got the right idea," he murmured, slipping her hands lower, to an even warmer spot.

Afraid to blink lest she discover she was in the midst of a dream, Nicky didn't close her eyes again.

Not when he kissed her.

Not when he drew her fingers—one at time—into his mouth. The sensual feel of his tongue sliding over her flesh made her quiver inside.

Voice husky, he said, "You're shaking again. I must be doing something wrong."

"Do it some more."

No shower could warm her the way he managed to do. He set her on fire. Fingers. Toes. Ears. Nose. And especially from the inside out.

When he braced her against the tile wall and finally entered her, Nicky tangled her fingers in the longish hair at his neck...thrust her tongue into his mouth...and wrapped her legs around his waist. She rocked him in long, smooth strokes to urge him faster and further.

"Easy," he murmured against her mouth. "We need to thaw you out slowly."

He demonstrated, drawing out the pleasure until it was nearly unbearable. No, Nicky thought. Unbearable would be Flint locked away or worse for something he didn't do.

Promising herself that wouldn't happen, she gave herself over to him completely.

FLINT REFUSED to let himself fall asleep with Nicky in his arms.

They'd made love a second time after eating dinner and toasting to new beginnings for a new year. Physically and emotionally exhausted, she'd gone out like a light. He'd held her until he began to feel sleepy, then had slipped off the futon and pulled on warm clothes. Ordering the dog to watch over her, he'd shrugged into his jacket and gloves, then had grabbed a flashlight before leaving the house.

He'd had hours to think about fate. Not only his.

Nicky had said something about hearing a noise before spinning out of control. He meant to take a closer look at the Pontiac, still prisoner of that tree.

The snow had stopped hours ago, and the new white blanket illuminated the area. His heart nearly stopped when he saw how precariously the heavy car clung to the slope. Had it gone into the river, things might have turned out differently.

Another tragedy.

Again using the rake as a staff, he carefully made his way down to the car, not knowing what to expect. A broken axle? When he shone the flashlight along the driver's side, he wasn't prepared for what he found.

The front tire had been slashed to ribbons.

Gut tightening, Flint climbed up to the garage and swept the area where the car had gone out of control. Though it must have been well camouflaged by the snow earlier, now the thing that had ripped the tire to shreds didn't take long to find.

Caught in the beam of his flashlight was a plank of wood studded with long, sharp nails.

A potentially fatal surprise...one that had been meant for him.

Chapter Thirteen

New Year's Day was half-gone by the time Nicky and Flint arrived at the ACT Legal Support Team offices via public transportation.

"You start checking for the license plate while I make a couple of calls," Flint told her. "I think I'll use Linda's office."

Nicky swallowed the lump that seemed to be blocking her throat. "Sure. Go ahead."

Another way to put some distance between them? she wondered, sadly watching him leave the room.

She'd awakened alone and had found Flint sacked out on the couch. Of course, he'd said he'd moved to the living room for her own good—he hadn't wanted to take a chance on hurting her. But all morning he'd been distracted. Kind of aloof. No heartfelt embraces or loving kisses after a night of passion. Even after the Pontiac had been towed to the local gas station, where the owner had assured Flint that his mechanic could get the boat up and running the very next day, he hadn't been himself.

Was he regretting making love to her already?

Comparing her to Alana and finding her lacking?

Nicky rubbed her right shoulder, which had stiffened during the night. She hated being so insecure, but she didn't know what else she was supposed to think. Thank goodness she hadn't spilled her guts and declared her love. Bad enough she'd admitted she needed him. Her only comfort was that he might think it had been a natural response to the situation.

But, bringing up the database, Nicky wondered how she was supposed to act around Flint now. Obviously not like his lover. And going back to their old relationship seemed impossible.

She got to work so that she wouldn't cry.

Calling up all combinations of license plate numbers starting with LTN 2, she set the parameters for the model and color, which left her with sixty-one candidates from the original nine hundred and ninety-nine. Then, still certain she'd seen a vanity plate, she looked for owners with the initials LTN. This search didn't pan out...no one even close. And yet those particular letters must have significance to the owner. If not the initials of his name, then something else. But what?

Puzzled, she scanned the entries one at a time, again eliminating addresses outside of Chicago and the surrounding suburbs. She was almost at the end of the run before coming to an entry that made her stop cold.

She knew then that LTN stood for Listen to the Night.

The owner of the silver Buick was Oren Maticek.

"I HAVEN'T TOLD Nicky what I found, because I don't want her going nuts on me," Flint explained to Phelps. "If she knew someone was trying to kill me, she wouldn't let me out of her sight."

Which presented him with a dilemma that had been

driving him crazy all morning. Would Nicky be safer away from him...or with him watching over her?

"If we had proof that someone tried to kill you—" Phelps was saying, "and a positive identity, of course—it would help your defense."

"How so?"

"We'd play on the possibility that the same person tried to kill you once before and failed. That Beverly Jensen was unlucky enough to intercept him and that's why she's dead."

"Sid Shelton." Flint quickly explained Nicky's theory about the man's quest for revenge. "He's the one most likely to have stolen Nicky's car to put her out of commission—on top of which he made a tidy profit. With Nicky's car gone, he'd have insurance that I'd be using the Pontiac. It makes sense, if in a convoluted way." And even if he had trouble believing it. "Now, how to prove it?"

"What did you do with the evidence?"

"Chucked it in the garbage."

Phelps groaned. "Let's hope it's still there so we can dust for fingerprints. How soon can you get it to me?"

"How soon do you want it?"

"I'll be home for the rest of the afternoon."

Flint signed off, promising that if he found the nail-studded board, it would be in the lawyer's hands as soon as he could get it there. A little sleuthing on his own was in order. He was trying to think up an excuse to leave Nicky in the safety of the office for a while when he realized she was standing in the doorway, staring at him.

"Have you been there long?"

"Not really."

Hoping it hadn't been long enough for her to have heard him talk about evidence, he asked, "You're finished with the search?"

"Done."

He figured she hadn't found anything if her downcast expression were any indication. And she was wearing her jacket.

"Going somewhere?"

"That's what I came to tell you. I just remembered I promised Mom I'd stop by this afternoon. You wouldn't want to come, would you?"

"Afraid not." Flint was relieved. She was giving him the perfect opportunity to retrieve the evidence without having to admit that her accident hadn't been one. "I don't know what else I can do here, so I might as well leave with you." He rose and snapped off the room lights. "We can grab a taxi, and I'll drop you off on my way home."

"Great."

They secured the premises and left. Waiting for the elevator, he said, "And you can meet me at my place later."

"I don't know. I'm kind of pooped. I thought I'd go home and crash."

Having decided that he would feel better if he could keep an eye on her—she tended to get herself in trouble alone—he asked, "And abandon Scraps?"

The dog was still at his place.

"Oops." The elevator doors opened. As they stepped into the empty car, she gave him a searching look. "There *is* Scraps to consider."

"And me."

"I figured you might be sick of my company by now."

"Never. Well, maybe doing things alone for short periods of time is okay. Absence makes the heart grow fonder," he joked, when what he really wanted to say was that he loved her and didn't want to let her out of his sight.

"So you want me to come by later?"

Flint suddenly realized she wasn't sure. And why should she be when he'd hardly paid her any mind all day? Not that he'd meant to make her feel abandoned.

"I *want you* to come by." And in case he didn't sound sincere enough, he decided a different sort of persuasion was in order. He took her in his arms and kissed her with tenderness and all the love that welled in his heart. "So what do you say?"

"That I'll be there?"

He kissed her again to make certain.

IN A MUCH BETTER MOOD—at least where Flint was concerned—Nicky waved to him as the taxi drove off. Ignoring her guilt at not telling him what she'd learned, she hurried up the front steps and rang the bell, which always felt odd considering she'd called the big old house home for most of her life.

Tension escalated with each unanswered ring. She had to warn her mother about her new beau. Where could she be? Hopefully, not with Oren Maticek. Maybe at a neighbor's...

Nicky ran down the steps and around to the back, intending to see if the Chevy was in the garage. If so, she would wait. She had to speak to her mother and *now.* She didn't like the feeling she was getting. Or the scary thoughts wandering into her head. She hated not telling Flint everything, but she wanted the opportunity to scope out the situation first. This was too important to let slide.

A quick peek through a grimy window into the darkened garage assured her the Chevy was there. Even as she turned away, she realized she'd glimpsed a second car beyond. But her mother only had one. Oren's? The silver Buick? Was her mother inside with him? No one answered the doorbell. What if her mother were in trouble? Heart pounding, she pressed her nose to the glass once again and squinted into the garage.

"Omigod! No."

Disbelieving, she backed away. Her chest tightened and she felt sick to her stomach.

Sid Shelton hadn't stolen her car, after all.

Nicky raced to the back porch and found the key hidden under a planter. Once inside, she crossed through the kitchen into the dining room, straight to the drawer where her mother kept spare keys. Including Nicky's. She and her mother had traded duplicates in case either of them was locked out.

From homes *or* cars.

Shoving several other sets aside, she grabbed the keys to the Escort. Now what? Should she leave, drive away and let her mother come to her? Or wait for as long as it took to demand an explanation? The decision was made for her when she heard a footstep and turned around to find her mother entering the room wearing a bathrobe, hair covered by a towel.

"Nicole! For heaven's sake! Are you trying to scare the life out of me?"

"I rang the doorbell several times."

"I didn't hear. I was in the shower."

"So I see."

Her mother's gaze dropped to the keys in Nicky's hand. Her eyes went wide and the color drained from her face. "Nicole?"

"I thought I'd drive my car home now, if that's all right with you."

"I—I can explain."

"Please do, Mom, because I can't imagine why you'd let your own daughter think her car was stolen!"

"I removed it for your own good."

"Is that what I should tell the police?"

"Police?" Cecilia grabbed onto the back of a chair for support. "You've involved the authorities?"

"What did you think I would do? My car was stolen!"

"Not stolen. I merely secured it for a while, but of course I planned to return it."

"Secured it why?"

"So *that man* wouldn't involve you in his troubles anymore."

Her fear escalated. "This *is* about Flint."

"No. I did it for you. Don't you see? I thought that if I kept your car for a few days, he couldn't take advantage of you driving him here and there. He'd have to get around on his own power. And then you would see he could do perfectly fine without you. It's as simple as that."

Nicky was appalled at her mother's reasoning. "It's not simple at all."

"You're my daughter, for heaven's sake, and I love you. I was afraid that if you didn't get away from him, you'd..." Cecilia closed her eyes and sucked in her breath. "I'm sorry. It's just that you've always been so willful. You've never listened to my advice." She put a hand to her heart. "A mother's love isn't always rational when she's trying to protect her child."

Nicky felt some of her anger dissipate. Hadn't she always longed for her mother's love and attention? The old saying "Be careful what you wish for" had merit.

"Mom, I'm an adult and I can make my own decisions."

"Please don't hold this against me." Voice quivering, her mother appeared frightened. "You're all I've got left in this world."

Nicky wanted to reassure her. But she couldn't. Not yet. "What else have you done?" She had to ask.

"Else?" Fine features pulling into a frown, Cecilia said, "Now *I* don't understand."

And maybe she didn't. Nicky wanted to believe her. She shifted. What was she thinking? Of course she believed her own mother.

"Don't worry about it."

"Then everything will be all right?"

Nicky nodded. "I'll figure out some story to set things straight with the police."

Like her mother had left her a message about borrowing her car, but that her answering machine was on the fritz...only that wouldn't wash with Flint. What was she going to tell *him?*

"Oh, Nicole."

Her mother put her arms around her and kissed her cheek.

Though she winced at the pain the hug caused her sore shoulder, Nicky caved completely.

Her mother's methods might be a little extreme, but she meant well. She was trying to protect her child.

Just as Nicky had sought out her mother to protect *her*.

Reminded of that, she said, "Mom, you have to stay away from Oren Maticek. He's big trouble."

"What?"

"I didn't want to scare you, so I didn't tell you that someone's been following me. Watching me."

Cecilia's green eyes widened. "What does that have to do with my Oren?"

"He drives a silver Buick—license plate LTN 2943. Listen to the Night is at 2943 Southport. When exactly did you meet Oren, Mom? And how?"

Lips trembling, she said, "The beginning of December. I received an invitation to visit the club, dinner and all on the house."

"Out of nowhere?"

"Oren said someone must have filled out a card with my name and address—a promotion to get new customers."

"And he approached you?"

"Yes, of course. A real lady never makes the first move."

Even worse. It occurred to her that Oren Maticek had arranged to meet her mother for nefarious purposes. She remembered asking about his businesses other than the club. She still had no answers.

"Mom, your new beau may be mixed up in Beverly Jensen's death somehow."

Cecilia sank down into a chair. She shook her head. Protested. "No. That's ridiculous."

"Then why has he been following me?"

"Oh, dear. That must be my fault, too. Oren is so very protective. A real gentleman from the old school. I'm afraid I voiced my concern for you more than once. He must have taken it to heart and decided to watch over you, thinking to please me. But I'll speak to him. I'll tell him to stop. I promise I will. Oren is a good man. *Please* let me handle this.''

Nicky was torn. What if Oren Maticek *had been* trying to protect her? She'd seen firsthand how her mother had been able to influence him. He'd seemed willing to do anything for ''his Ceci.'' And what had he really done that she knew of? He wasn't the one who'd stolen her car.

Though she was troubled by her decision, she agreed in the end. Not that Flint would agree if *he* knew.

Sick inside, Nicky wished there were some way she could be honest with him and still remain loyal to her mother.

NICKY WAITED until she and Flint were having their after-dinner coffee in the living room before fetching the present she'd brought with her. She removed the gaily wrapped package from the bag and held it out.

''I thought maybe you were ready for this. Besides, the tree has to come down this weekend, so what was I going to do with it? Come on.''

Flint hesitated only a second before taking it from her. ''I still didn't get you one.''

''You're present enough for me.''

His smile broke her heart. Being torn between the two people she loved most was a dilemma that had no safe resolution. Fearing she would lose Flint over it, she determined to savor every moment with him. As he opened the package, she noted his expression softened the moment he saw what was inside.

''Megan.''

"I thought you might like to have it."

Shortly before they'd moved, she'd taken almost an entire roll of film of father and daughter playing together outside. She loved this particular shot of the two of them, happy smiles wreathing their faces as Flint caught Megan in a bear hug from behind. She'd had it blown up and had bought a special keepsake frame with the word *remember* carved into the wood in several places.

He touched the photo as if reaching out for his daughter. "I need to remember her," he admitted, his features growing grim. "Megan was everything to me. She was what I lived for." He swallowed hard. "I've hardly been able to think about her. Not when I'm responsible...she's dead because of me."

"Because of an act of nature."

"I couldn't save her. After I found Alana, I went into Megan's room, but I couldn't get to her in time."

Nicky's heart skipped a beat. "She was alive?" He'd never mentioned it before. How horrible for him.

"She had to be. I heard her calling to me. I know I did." His fingers visibly tightened around the frame. "I tried to get to her, but everything collapsed...I couldn't dig her out. I never saw her, but I can still hear her whispering, 'Daddy.'" He reached for her hand and squeezed. "Thank you for this, Nicky. I'll treasure it always."

Her eyes filled with tears. His pain was so obvious. She imagined he didn't even have a sense of closure. That had to be why he'd refused to enter Megan's room since returning from California. In his heart, he knew his child was dead, but he hadn't been able to see for himself. He hadn't been able to hold her one last time. Even her casket had been closed.

"Why didn't you ever say anything?" she asked, nearly choking on the words.

"How does a father admit he failed his child so completely?"

He was in agony. The way her mother had been over her? She was doing the right thing, Nicky told herself.

As Flint set the frame on a shelf visible from anywhere in the room, he said, "You had a point about my needing to work this out with a professional."

"Did something happen that I don't know about?" she asked, imagining she hit a nerve.

He recovered quickly. "*You* happened. You forced me to wake up and see what I was missing. Life."

Words to warm her heart. "I'm glad I did something right."

She only hoped he would never find out about her mother and Oren, that he would never know she was holding back. He had no idea the Escort was in her possession. She'd parked it on a side street near her building and had walked over.

"I'm going to call Dr. Galloway tomorrow. She suggested I might be able to overcome the sleepwalking episodes."

"I'm sure you can."

"If I'm not locked up first."

"That's not going to happen. Not with her testifying on your behalf." Believing that he had the best defense possible—that he would walk away from the trial a free man—was the only way she could live with herself. "I've been thinking."

"About?"

"Our investigation—it's going nowhere."

"These things take time."

"But we've been putting in a full-time effort for nearly a week and what do we have to show for it?"

"Maybe more than you know," he suggested.

More than *he* knew, that was for certain. Guilt ate at her, but she couldn't help herself. Her mother had only gotten involved because of her. And Oren because of her mother. If she ceased and desisted, so would they. No sense in exposing them for no good reason.

"I just can't see us going on like this...wasting our time."

Flint frowned. "That's a strange turnaround for the person who forced me to take action."

"I know. I guess I've come to my senses. Sorry for bullying you."

Though she wasn't sorry that their searching for the truth had brought him out of his self-imposed isolation. Or that it had brought them together. Surely if he *did* learn what she was hiding down the line, she could make him understand why she'd done so.

"I'm taking my life back," Flint said. "I'm not about to give up now."

Making Nicky's mouth go dry. She hadn't expected this. "But you have an excellent defense." She was trying to convince herself as well as him.

"But I don't know that it's the truth. What if you've been right all along and I had nothing to do with Beverly's death? A killer may be on the loose, walking the streets. Besides which, I need the truth more than anything."

More than her? A lump seemed to fill her throat. "I can't help you anymore."

Flint stiffened. "I thought we were in this together."

"I do have to take care of other things in my life," she reminded him. "School is back in session in a few days. I have to prepare for classes."

Their combined silence was louder than any argument. The space between them seemed to grow and multiply by leaps and bounds until she lost any sense of connection. She felt as if she were staring at a stranger.

Finally, Flint said, "Then maybe you should get started."

The sick feeling welled up in her again. She joked, "You're kicking me out?"

His tone was deadly serious when he said, "I wouldn't want to waste any more of your time."

Nicky was stunned. He *was* serious. Not knowing what else to do, she found her jacket and, taking Scraps with her, left without another word.

Flint didn't try to stop her.

Tears choked her as she rushed down the street. She'd wanted Flint to care about life again. Now he did.

How could she have known something so positive would be a double-edged sword for her?

"DADDY..."

A faint cry...real or imagined?

The shadow of Megan's bed stood amid the debris. "Daddy?"

To his horror, what was left of her room was swallowed whole by another quake. Bare-handed, he savaged the ever-shifting rubble.

"Megan, honey, Daddy's here! Don't be afraid! I'll get you out, I promise!"

*He dug and dug, working like a madman until his
hands were raw and his mind numb....*

Until he made contact with warm, vibrant flesh.

"Megan, I've got you!" he choked out.

A sense of elation filled him. He grabbed with both
hands, resolving not to let go until he had his child in
his arms again. Until he could see her beloved little
face.

With a start, Flint realized he was awake...out of
bed...sleepwalking again.

And again, he wasn't alone.

Rolling around on the living room floor, he deter-
minedly held on to the intruder who was pummeling
him, even when they banged into an end table, sending
it crashing....

NICKY STARED UP into the dark, knowing what she had
to do. She checked the clock. A little after two. The
middle of the night. What did it matter?

Climbing out of bed, she switched on a light and
found the clothes she'd dumped on a chair.

Awake as well, Scraps sat up and yawned.

"Sorry, boy, not this time. I've got to go alone.
Flint deserves the truth."

She'd had hours to think it over. She couldn't fail
him, couldn't hold back one iota of what she'd
learned—not even if he hated her for it. His life was
at stake. Her mother's wasn't.

Besides, how did she know her mother wasn't mistaken about Oren?

Worse, how did she know her mother hadn't been
manipulating *her* as she'd done so successfully with
Alana?

Had her need for her mother's love made her gullible?

Five minutes and she was ready to leave. She didn't take her car—not because she meant to hide its recovery from Flint any longer, but because the cold air would clear her head.

And the walk would give her a few extra minutes to work up her courage.

Arriving at Flint's front door, Nicky was about to ring the bell until she heard a crash. He was sleepwalking again. She didn't hesitate to use the keys Alana had given her to check on the house when they'd left for California.

Keys...

Unlocking the door, she realized she'd seen duplicates of these among the others in her mother's drawer.

Another crash added to the noise of a struggle made her flip on the living room lights. To her shock, Flint was locked in silent combat.

And his attacker was Eric Jensen.

Chapter Fourteen

"Nicky, get out of here!" Flint yelled. "Run!"

Already picking up the phone, she ignored the command and dialed 911.

"Let go, Armstrong!" Jensen growled.

Nicky watched in horror as he elbowed the man she loved in the face. "Stop that!"

But Flint gave as good as he got. Still hanging on to Jensen with his left hand, he managed a potent punch with his right.

And Nicky realized she'd gotten through. "Murderer!" she gasped. "We've got him! Hurry."

Her request was punctuated by the crash of a vase toppling. She gave the emergency operator the address and dropped the receiver without hanging up. Flint's face was smeared with blood and he seemed unable to hang on to Jensen. Frantic, she looked around for a weapon. She ripped the cord of a halogen floor lamp from the wall and mistakenly grabbed the pole. Her sore shoulder quickly protested as she tried to lift it.

Flint tripped the other man, who was trying to get away. Jensen staggered facefirst into the wall. Flint bounded to his feet, grabbed the dazed man by collar and belt and whipped him, stomach down, across the back of the couch, where he checked him for a weapon.

"You're not going anywhere until you tell the cops why and how you murdered your ex-wife."

"Putting on a show for *her?*"

"Leave Nicky out of this. It's you and me, Jensen."

"Yeah! I should've taken you out weeks ago. Then the only woman I ever loved would still be alive."

Letting go of the lamp, Nicky got close enough to smell the alcohol on Jensen. He was drunk again.

"You picked the wrong night, though," she said. "Beverly was here, and she's the one who died."

"*He* killed her, not me. Christ, let me up before I puke all over your couch."

"Don't try anything." Flint backed off, letting Jensen straighten.

Nicky pursued the truth. "Did you get drunk at that Christmas Eve party," she asked, "or on your way here?"

"You're not pinning Bev's death on me when *he's* the one who killed her."

He said it as though he believed it, Nicky realized, even as Jensen bolted for the front door. Flint stopped him, whirling him around and throwing him into an armchair.

"What are you doing here tonight?" he asked. "Were you planning to make good on your threat against me? Or did you just want to see if the car did the job for you?"

"What car?" Nicky asked, realization making her breath catch. "Not the Pontiac."

"The accident you had last night...was no accident."

Suddenly feeling weak-kneed, heat engulfing her

with the knowledge that she'd survived a murder attempt, she removed her jacket and took a few deep breaths. Absently, she rubbed her shoulder.

"And it's no coincidence that our friend shows up here tonight," Flint added.

"What the hell are you talking about!" Jensen shouted.

"Again, you miscalculated. It was Nicky who was driving when the tire went. You almost killed her, too."

"You're crazy!"

"I have proof. Or rather my lawyer does."

"What proof? Why were you keeping it from me?" Nicky demanded before realizing she was as guilty of keeping secrets as he.

Jensen licked his lips. He had the air of a wild animal about him. Desperate. Trapped.

"I watched you a few times, yeah," he admitted. "I even thought about ways to make you pay for Bev's death. But I never did anything about it, I swear!"

"You broke into my house tonight. Why? To wish me a Happy New Year?"

Jensen was shaking his head. "The back door was already open."

"I made sure the locks were drawn before I went to bed."

"Then whoever came in here before I did has a key."

Nicky's pulse surged. "You're saying someone else is in this house?" Knowing of only one other person who had a key, she felt sick inside.

"Yeah. I saw someone sneaking around and followed...hell, I don't even know what I thought I was going to do.''

A wooden board creaked. Nicky whipped around toward the staircase.

A lump in her throat, she said, ''You might as well come down.'' When she got no response, she added, ''The police are on their way.''

''You said you weren't going to call them, Nicole.''

''Cecilia?'' Flint seemed startled...and wary.

Cecilia Keating descended several stairs, gun in hand. The barrel was pointed at Flint's chest, and Nicky knew she *had* been a gullible fool. Her heart felt as if it had just been ripped in two.

''Mom, put the gun down.''

''Too late now. You broke your promise.''

Realizing her mother wasn't stable and might shoot someone without meaning to, Nicky knew it was up to her to diffuse the situation. She drew closer.

''I called the police because this man was trespassing and attacking Flint,'' she explained far more calmly than she was feeling. ''Eric Jensen.''

''That woman's husband.'' Stopped halfway down the staircase, Cecilia focused on him. ''So she was cheating on you just like *that man* was cheating on my Alana.''

''Mom, Alana's dead!''

''Is that why you decided to kill Beverly?'' Flint asked.

''If anyone should be dead, it's you!'' Pure hatred shone from her eyes. ''Alana was everything to me, and you took her away! First from my home...then from this city...finally from life itself.''

''She was my wife. Getting her away from you was my last chance to save my marriage.''

"How dare you—"

"Speak the truth? That's more than you've been doing."

"Your seeing another woman, sleeping with her in Alana's house, in Alana's bed, was more than I could bear! I came here to see for myself, to tell you what I thought of you." Her expression changed to one of puzzlement. "But you weren't in the master bedroom where you were supposed to be. I was coming down the stairs when your harlot caught me and had the nerve to demand to know what *I* was doing here. I told her she was an adulteress and that she should be ashamed of herself. She was going to wake you, tell you what a crazy old woman I was. *Old!* Can you imagine her saying that to *me?* I tried to stop her...she fell and hit her head."

"In the dining room," Nicky said, ignoring the bile that rose to her throat. "How did she get in Flint's bed?"

"I dragged her there, of course. Alana always said not even an earthquake would waken that man. And to my everlasting grief, she was correct."

Nicky stared at her mother, who was obviously far more disturbed than she'd ever realized. "You purposely framed Flint for murder."

"I only wanted justice. He took Alana away from me. And then he tried to take you. You're all I have left, Nicole. I can't lose you, too."

No. She couldn't lose the afterthought who'd had no value until the treasured daughter was out of her reach. Eyes filling with tears, Nicky took a step up.

"You lied to me this afternoon."

"For your own good."

"What about Oren? Did you lie about him, too? What did you get him to do for you?"

For all she knew, he could be outside, waiting for her mother.

"I only asked him to keep an eye on you because I feared for your life hanging around that man so much. Paying those gang members was Oren's idea. He thought if they scared you enough, you'd stop."

"You put your own daughter in danger?"

"Of course not. You weren't hurt."

"I was hurt last night when the Pontiac crashed," Nicky said, taking another step up. "I'm lucky to be alive. I may owe my life to Flint."

Her mother's forehead furrowed. "You? But you weren't supposed to be in that car."

"I was parking it when it went over the embankment. What if I'd been killed? How would you justify murdering your own daughter?"

Confusion played across her mother's face. Nicky saw her opportunity. She started to take another step.

"Nicky, don't."

Flint's low warning made her hesitate until her mother held the gun out at him, saying, "This is your fault!" Though she tried steadying the weapon with both hands, the barrel quivered.

Taking the next step, Nicky said, "Mom, you can't shoot anyone."

"I have to or I'll go mad!"

Nicky rushed up the remaining few stairs, determined to disarm her. But when she reached out, excruciating pain shot through her shoulder and she faltered, merely jostling the gun with her hand rather than securing it.

"No, Nicole, no!"

Her mother's warning punctuated a loud crack and flash. Heat seared Nicky, effectively stopping her.

"My God!" Flint cried from behind her.

With disbelief, she touched the blood spreading across the middle of her sweater. Tears finally rolling down her cheeks, she met her mother's panicked gaze and held out her bloody hand. "Look what you did to me, Mom."

"An accident, Nicole, I swear!"

Sobbing, her mother dropped the gun and reached for her, even as Nicky felt strong hands steady and lift her from behind.

"I've got you," Flint murmured, lips in her hair. "Cecilia, stay away from her!"

Everything went blurry as all feeling faded and she began to go limp.

"No, Nicole, don't die! You can't leave me!"

Her mother's screech was the last thing Nicky heard as her world went from bloodred to black.

THE LUMP BLOCKING Flint's throat felt too big to swallow as he stared down at Nicky's pale face. He sat on the edge of her hospital bed, holding her limp hand. Having made it through a difficult if successful surgery, she was connected to a tube that brought her vital fluids and medications from several bags.

"Come back to me, Nicky. I'm going crazy waiting for you. That instant gratification need of yours seems to be contagious."

He'd been talking to her on and off for hours to no result. His patience was wearing thin. Though the doctors had assured him she was going to be as good as new, he wouldn't believe it until he could look into her eyes to see for himself that she was all right.

Suddenly, he realized he was doing just that. Those blue eyes had to be the most beautiful sight in the world.

"Thank God. You're awake."

"And you're here," she whispered.

"Where else would I be but at the side of the woman I love?"

She tried adjusting her position, but stopped midstream, her face squinching.

Flint felt her pain. "Where are you hurting?"

"All over... What happened?" She swallowed hard and a bleak expression swept her beloved face. "My own mother shot me."

"She didn't mean to hurt you, Nicky," Flint said. "I do believe that. And that's what I told the police. They were just leaving their squad car when they heard the gunshot. After that, everything happened so fast. I might have been taken in and booked if it weren't for Eric Jensen. He got me off the hook both for your being shot and for Beverly's death. The charges against me have already been dropped."

"I'm so glad." She gave him more of a grimace than a smile. "What about Mom?"

So like Nicky to worry about others before herself. She didn't even ask about her own prognosis.

"I convinced Phelps to represent Cecilia. He's trying to decide how to plead—whether to factor in her diminished mental capacity or to go with accidental death. Either way, we'll see that your mother finally gets the help she's needed for years."

Her relief was clear when she said, "You're amazing. You did that for her, after all she's put you through."

"I didn't do it for her," Flint clarified. "I did it for *you*."

"Because you love me?" She sounded as if she needed to be convinced.

"So much it hurts. That's your fault, by the way, because you made me feel again. Everything has changed for me in the past week," he admitted. "You bullied me into wanting to live again. Really live. Preferably, with you."

"I was so afraid I was just an Alana substitute to you…that you were somehow mixing me up with her like Mom did."

While he longed to take Nicky in his arms, Flint didn't want to cause her more physical pain. He contented himself stroking her cheek and smoothing the hair from her forehead.

"Cecilia might have seen her relationship with you as what she needed to fill the gap in her life," he said, "but I believe she loves you and in her own warped way, was trying to protect you. And I don't think she ever confused you with Alana. I know I never did."

"You didn't? You're sure?"

"Positive. You're nothing like your sister." He didn't want to badmouth a dead woman—especially not one that he had loved in the beginning—so all he said in the way of explanation was, "It takes more than beauty, charm and good intentions to keep a relationship going. The truth is our marriage was on the rocks, but I was determined to find a way to make it stick. I had a daughter to think about. I didn't want to walk out on Megan like your father did to you and Alana."

"You never would have walked out on Megan even

if you and Alana had divorced," Nicky said with certainty. "That's not who you are."

"And Alana is not who *you* are." Thankfully. "You're your own person, and a very special one at that. You have a bigger heart than anyone I've ever met. And I want to call it mine, Nicky. I never thought I could love a woman as much as I do you. I don't know how to live without you anymore."

"I hope that's an exaggeration."

Flint swallowed hard. Had he misread her, then? "Because you don't feel the same way?"

"Because I don't ever want to see you caught in the depths of guilt and despair the way you were before. That would break my heart."

The numbness he'd experienced for so long suddenly seemed far in the past, no matter that it had been mere days. Uncertain of what might have happened to him had Nicky died, Flint knew he would have to guard against the return of such apathy. Giving up on life for any reason was simply unacceptable.

"I'll be working with Dr. Galloway on the sleeping disorder and underlying causes. I'm going to lick it, Nicky. So what do you say about us?"

Tears shone in her eyes, but Nicky was smiling. And a weight lifted from Flint's soul.

"I say that I fell in love with you the day you walked into our house. What I thought was a teenage crush turned out to be the real thing. I've loved you all along, Flint, and you won't have to go it alone. I'll fight alongside you...if that's not too controlling."

Flint grinned. His Nicky was back, quirky humor and all.

"Exactly what I hoped you'd say," he murmured, then kissed her to seal the bargain.

Epilogue

"Any questions? Alex?"

Snapping back to the present, Alex realized Zoe was waiting for his response. "I'm sorry...."

"I wanted to know if you had any questions before starting to work on this chapter."

"Only one." But an important one. One that he could relate to. "Was Flint really able to overcome the inner conflicts that drove him to such apathy?"

"If Dr. Galloway's reports are to be believed, yes." Zoe's delicate brow cleared and she began gathering her materials together. "That doesn't mean he won't be haunted by such a terrible tragedy at times, but he's been able to put what happened in perspective, and more important, to stop blaming himself."

"That's great," Alex said, feeling better than he had in a long time. Maybe there was hope for him, as well. He'd never guessed that writing a book on the Seven Deadly Sins would be a kind of therapy. "Good for him."

And for an outcome that gave him hope for himself.

KEY TO MY HEART

Unlock the secrets of romance just in time for the most romantic day of the year—Valentine's Day!

Key to My Heart
features three of your favorite authors,

**Kasey Michaels,
Rebecca York
and Muriel Jensen,**

to bring you wonderful tales of romance and Valentine's Day dreams come true.

As an added bonus you can receive Harlequin's special Valentine's Day necklace. FREE with the purchase of every *Key to My Heart* collection.

Available in January,
wherever Harlequin books are sold.

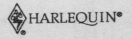 HARLEQUIN®

PHKEY349

Coming in August 1997!

THE BETTY NEELS
RUBY COLLECTION

August 1997—Stars Through the Mist
September 1997—The Doubtful Marriage
October 1997—The End of the Rainbow
November 1997—Three for a Wedding
December 1997—Roses for Christmas
January 1998—The Hasty Marriage

COLLECTOR'S EDITION

This August start assembling the
Betty Neels Ruby Collection. Six of the
most requested and best-loved titles have
been especially chosen for this collection.
From August 1997 until January 1998,
one title per month will be available to avid
fans. Spot the collection by the lush ruby red
cover with the gold Collector's Edition banner
and your favorite author's name—Betty Neels!

Available in August at your favorite retail outlet.

HARLEQUIN®

Look us up on-line at: http://www.romance.net

BNRUBY

HARLEQUIN®

INTRIGUE®

Winner of the prestigious
Reviewer's Choice Award

Kelsey Roberts

invites you to drop in anytime to

THE ROSE TATTOO

Welcome to Charleston's hottest restaurant,
featuring Southern specialties with a side order of
mystery and an extra helping of romance. There,
excitement and passion are always on the menu.

**Look for Kelsey Roberts's latest
ROSE TATTOO...**

#455 HER MOTHER'S ARMS
Coming in February!

Look us up on-line at: http://www.romance.net   HINR455

HARLEQUIN®

I N T R I G U E®

When little Adam Kingsley was taken from his nursery in the Kingsley mansion, the Memphis family used all their power and prestige to punish the kidnapper. They believed the crime was solved and the villain condemned...though the boy was never returned. But now, new evidence comes to light that may reveal the truth about...

The Kingsley Baby

Amanda Stevens is at her best for this powerful trilogy of a sensational crime and the three couples whose love lights the way to the truth. Don't miss:

#453 THE HERO'S SON (February)
#458 THE BROTHER'S WIFE (March)
#462 THE LONG-LOST HEIR (April)

What *really* happened that night in the Kingsley nursery?

Look us up on-line at: http://www.romance.net

HINKING

DEBBIE MACOMBER

invites you to the

HEART OF TEXAS

Join Debbie Macomber as she brings you the lives and loves of the folks in the ranching community of Promise, Texas.

If you loved Midnight Sons—don't miss Heart of Texas! A brand-new six-book series from Debbie Macomber.

Available in February 1998 at your favorite retail store.

Heart of Texas by Debbie Macomber

Lonesome Cowboy	February '98
Texas Two-Step	March '98
Caroline's Child	April '98
Dr. Texas	May '98
Nell's Cowboy	June '98
Lone Star Baby	July '98

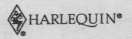

HARLEQUIN®

HPHRT1

HARLEQUIN®
INTRIGUE®

In the mountains of Colorado, the snow comes in on a gust of wind, reaching blizzard conditions in a matter of minutes. Here, the Rampart Mountain Rescue Team is never lonely. But this year there's even more activity than usual for the team, as not only Mother Nature but mystery is swirling in their midst.

Rocky Mtn. RESCUE

Join three of your favorite Intrigue authors for an intimate look at the lives and loves of the men and women of one of America's highest mountain rescue teams. It's the place to be for thrills, chills and adventure!

Don't miss

**#449 FORGET ME NOT by Cassie Miles
January 1998**

**#454 WATCH OVER ME by Carly Bishop
February 1998**

**#459 FOLLOW ME HOME by Leona Karr
March 1998**

Look us up on-line at: http://www.romance.net   HINRMR

MURDER, BLACKMAIL AND LIES...

Suspicion

A young law clerk is killed. A high-priced call girl is strangled. Two men are accused of their murders. And defense attorney Kate Logan intends to prove their innocence—even though the evidence and witnesses say otherwise. With the help of homicide detective Mitch Calhoun, Kate discovers evidence suggesting that the two cases may be connected. But when her life and the life of her daughter are threatened, Kate and Mitch realize they have stumbled into a maze of corruption and murder...where no one is above suspicion.

CHRISTIANE HEGGAN

"A master at creating taut, romantic suspense." —*Literary Times*

MIRA BOOKS

Available January 1998
at your favorite retail outlet.

Look us up on-line at: http://www.romance.net

MCH305